L♥VE HATES VIOLENCE

VIOLENCE

The Twisted Truth

DE'WAYNE MARIS

GOOD 2 GO PUBLISHING

Community Library of DeWitt & Jamesville
5110 Jamesville Road
DeWitt, NY 13078

LOVE HATES VIOLENCE

Written by DE'WAYNE MARIS

Cover Design: Davida Baldwin – Odd Ball Designs

Typesetter: Mychea

ISBN: 9781947340268

Copyright © 2018 Good2Go Publishing

Published 2018 by Good2Go Publishing

7311 W. Glass Lane • Laveen, AZ 85339

www.good2gopublishing.com

https://twitter.com/good2gobooks

G2G@good2gopublishing.com

www.facebook.com/good2gopublishing

www.instagram.com/good2gopublishing

ACKNOWLEDGEMENTS

Hey, Mom, my dearest lady. I love you and thank you for having me. I know I made mistakes in life, but I hope that my accomplishments make up for that.

Shaun, Nicole, Anthony, Donnie, Lil Gween, Key, Dezhahal, Saniyah, Kizzy (the Real Jai), and the rest of my fam, I love y'all. And for all my dawgz locked down—Lil Woody, Chub, Sheldon, and all the rest—who read my script and pushed me to the fullest 'cause they saw something in me, good lookin'. And, Chris Cobb, ya know what it is—it's all love. Send mines to the dawg.

Also, I wanna say what's up to the O'Neal fam and Chucky. Love y'all. And, Flower, give Jaylen and Makayla a hug for me. Love y'all. And last but certainly not least, I want to thank G2Go Publishing for giving me a chance to shine . . . highly appreciated.

And to all my readers out there, I got some more work in the makings. So if you dig this one, then stay posted. It's on its way.

And to anyone reading this that shouldn't, it was just all a figment of my imagination . . . the art of writing.

Thank you!

I t was the summer of 2006. The sun was out with clear blue skies. It was beach weather for those that lived in Southern California. It was about ninety degrees outside, but the news predicted that it would reach the triple digits some time later.

The community was out and about enjoying the summer breeze with their daily shopping at the supermarkets, getting their cars washed, or just relaxing at the parks while watching the little ones play in the sandbox. Dogs barked as sidewalkers passed gated yards with Beware of Dog signs on the gates, hoping they were locked.

There were no major worries in the city as people carried on with their daily rituals. Wish the same could have been said for the residents of Chino, California, who lived near the Bank of America which sat in a small shopping mall that was now surrounded with patrol cars and officers with guns drawn.

The neighborhood had been ordered on lockdown as they now had one suspect held up in a house with one hostage.

The standoff lasted twelve hours while SWAT attempted to negotiate with the man inside, but he refused to give up.

Suddenly, shots rang out as officers took cover behind their patrol cars. It was time to move in. The SWAT team bombarded the house with tear gas and sting lights to temporarily blind anyone who was inside, in order to take down the suspect.

Shots rang out again as the agents fired multiple times, hitting the armed suspect in the torso and dropping him immediately.

"Clear!" one agent yelled while another agent escorted the hostage out, who was slightly dazed from all the drama.

"Target is down!" another agent yelled into his radio, kicking the gun from the motionless body.

He knelt down over the suspect to check for a pulse, but changed his mind once he saw the huge hole just below the heart gushing out blood.

"This one's gone!" he said through the radio. "Send the coroner."

* * *

Heath woke up in the hospital hooked up to all kinds of tubes running from his body to a machine. The sounding beeps kept track of his heart rate, which was steady for the time being.

After the coroner had come and zipped him up in a body bag, the doctor was shocked to have found a pulse just before the autopsy as

Heath's body lay on the table. He immediately called for a bus to take him to the nearest hospital for treatment after calling law enforcement. Heath now lay in the hospital bed while cuffed, waiting to get well so that he could answer to the charges of bank robbery, kidnapping, and a host of other charges.

In his dreams, Heath knew something was wrong. He kept feeling himself ripped away from the lifestyle he loved so much: the parties, the club scene with strippers and their booties poppin', and the money. Oh, how much he loved them big faces. Heath lived for that, sold drugs for that, and sometimes even killed for it. And from looking at his situation right now, Heath seemed to die for it.

His boys had told him to stay away from that bank money. They tried to show him another way of life, one that didn't create too much attention. And the payout was just as much. He did it for a while and even enjoyed it, but each time he came back to the States, he would go on his missions of robbing banks. He didn't know why he did it; he didn't need the money. But his boy and crime boss, Iron'RE, kept his pockets lined up.

Iron'RE lived a lifestyle of those you saw in mafia flicks or read books about. He had an operation that expanded to all four corners of the earth. A know hirer, Iron'RE was always looking for some soldiers to do a hit for him. He ran into Heath by way of a friend named Que; and as their work grew, so did their friendship. Yet Heath always felt that he was missing something.

Heath had never gotten the love that he deserved while growing up. His mother was never around, even to the point that he couldn't tell it was her if he saw her.

He was raised by his grandmother the first quarter of his life, while spending the rest in the streets chasing the same dreams once pursued by the man that he called his father. Heath knew him by another name and title. And ever since he laid eyes on him, he knew that he wanted to be just like him. But little did he know at the time that his very blood was already pumping in his veins.

So here he was now, a rendition of his pops long ago, strapped to a bed with IVs and machines sustaining his life. But the only difference was that his pops never made it.

Pops was the AK-47 bandit who had the same motives as Heath. He robbed every bank in Chino, California—only he never left witnesses. His pops spent his money just as fast as he got it, splurging on fancy rides, Harley bikes, and clothes.

Never once did he think about putting something to the side, snatching his son up and introducing him to the realities of life. He never turned him on to other things that mattered like stocks and bonds, buying and selling properties, or getting a nice woman to settle down with. Nah, Heath wasn't up on that. He wanted it quick; and just like his pops, he had no regard for anyone—nobody at all— until now. Now shit had just gotten real!

His eyes came alive, and at that very moment, he spotted the image that he was sure he left in hell down by the fire, which caused him torment during his brief hibernation.

He jumped when he saw the corn-fed sheriff sitting in a chair in the corner of the room with eyes locked on his bedridden body like a trained assassin.

"Shoot the bastard if he tries anything! He should've been dead. If he moves, makes sure there's no trial," were the instructions from the captain.

The officer waited and even played dirty by uncuffing Heath from the bed while he was still out. The officer hoped that Heath would make a move so that he could pop him and say that he had gone for his service weapon, just like some other officers in LA suggested when trying to justify the shooting and killing of an innocent black man.

Despite the drugs and the IV, Heath could never forget the look on the officer's face.

"Go on, see what happens!" the look in the officer's eyes seemed to say.

Although he was still wounded and in pain, Heath sat up just enough to raise his arms with a smirk on his face. He took one arm to grab the cuffs with his hand in order to cuff himself back to the bed.

"Not today, skinhead!" Heath said in a muffled voice.

"What's that? What did ya say?" the officer asked as he leaned in close, so close that Heath could smell his stinky cologne and bad breath.

"Nothin', man!" Heath replied, looking at the officer. "What the fuck happened? I thought I died. What the fuck you save me for?"

The officer just looked at him and smiled.

Heath lay back down on the bed and screamed until the pain started to come back. The bandage around his chest began to turn red from the blood that gushed from the wound, and then he passed out.

The blood spread like a wildfire as straight lines appeared on the screen of one of the machines that kept track of his heart beat. Nurses came running in screaming.

"We got a flatline!"

They tried to resuscitate Heath as the officer stood over him screaming for him to die.

"Die, you piece of shit! Do us all a favor!"

* * *

Heath noticed that the courtroom was just as cold as the hospital. It had been a long time since he last saw a room like this one—a room filled with Americanized artifacts of the judicial system. And never in his wildest dreams did he think he would be here again, he thought as the bailiff escorted him to his seat in county blues while shackled from the waist down.

A few minutes ago he was still in a wheelchair recovering from the chest wound that SWAT had given him, which almost took his life. In fact, he wished the attacked was successful.

"Why didn't they just go for the head?" he thought to himself as he turned around to look at the faces of civilians that had come to support their loves one.

He didn't see anyone familiar, so he turned back around to face the judge.

Heath smirked at the name plate that hung just below him, and he thought to himself, "I must be having buzzard luck, to be going in front of a judge with a name like Hatchett!"

Just then, his attorney walked in and placed her briefcase on the table. She wore a blue blazer over a cream-colored blouse tucked into her miniskirt that fell just above her knees, which rose a few inches as she sat down, exposing the thickness of her thighs.

Heath tried not to look, but his eyes were followed by hers as she leaned in to introduce herself.

Her name was Ms. Gentry, a highly recommended attorney for his type of case.

You could never tell from the glamorous look and urban accent that his ghetto beauty had been the reason for multiple acquittals, retrials, and not-guilty verdicts. If forties were the new twenties, you would think that Ms. Gentry had about twenty years of experience at being a woman.

"Good morning, Mr. Heath! Iron'RE has retained me as your attorney. He has instructed me to inform you to keep your head up and not to worry," she began before briefly going over the case.

She reassured him that there was not too much that could make the case stick, just an eyewitness to say that she saw him fleeing from the scene with a gun.

"What was this lady smoking?" he questioned to himself.

He wanted to jump up and pull his shirt off so she could see the huge hole in his chest caused by the SWAT team that he was sure was coming to trial, if there was one, to tell their version of what had happened. Or what about the thirteen-year-old who just happened to be home alone when he busted through the back door?

"Man, this broad's on dope, dick, and dynamite if she thinks I'm going on trial!" he thought to himself.

He decided to take the deal and call it a wrap. He told the attorney, but she protested, thinking that she could somehow still win the case. Heath made a mental note to tell Iron'RE to fire her the first chance he got, and not to worry about him. He needed some time away. In fact, that's what he told Iron'RE the first chance he got. But for now, he waited on the judge to agree on the plea deal of ten years.

"Ohmar Heath Jackson, I sentence you to do your time at the Lompoc Federal Prison. It seems from your extensive background that you are no stranger to the penal system. And judging from your actions and your acceptance of this plea bargain, it has become evident that you have accepted your destiny. I wish you luck."

Heath couldn't believe what had just happened. How in the world could he be going back to prison? He had already spent six months in the downtown Federal jail going back and forth to court, which seemed like an eternity. His attorney took it all in stride, turning to him with a reassuring look on her face.

"Don't worry. Stay strong!" she said.

Heath wasn't trying to hear all that. He searched the courtroom and looked for loved ones just like before, but all he could see were the faces of strangers.

He wanted to flip the table over when his attorney got up to leave. She turned around and put her hand on his shoulder to try to ease whatever it was that was going through his brain.

"Don't worry, Heath, this is what I do. You're a good friend of Iron'RE. I'll do something to get you out of here. Just be good!"

She waved to the bailiff and let him know that her client was ready to go back to his cell. As he got up, he looked a last time at the faces behind him.

"Ain't this a bitch!" he thought at the sight of not one familiar face.

L♥VE HATES VIOLENCE

VIOLENCE

The Twisted Truth

The water was lukewarm. Bubbles began to dissipate as he relaxed in the tub. He often took long bubble baths after a good workout at the gym as a form of relaxation.

For the past couple of months, Heath had found himself struggling with the fact that he had been out of prison a year now and was still alone. He had no problem finding a chick, but the problem was finding the right one.

He lived alone in his family-sized condo, which sat along Belmont Shores in Long Beach. He was a bachelor and eye candy to just about every female beachgoer within the proximity of his front door.

He jumped out of the tub, refusing to grab a towel and letting the water drip from his chiseled body while admiring himself in the mirror. It was day 366, one year and a day since he was released from the "Belly of the Beast"—a place that some people liked to call prison.

His reflection responded with a smile of satisfaction, exuberant due to the fact that he had just survived a whole year without any trouble with the law, giving him a reason to celebrate that night.

* * *

The sun was beginning to disappear into the hills of Palo Verde as the burned orange pierced the sky. A perfect view, he thought as he looked at the harbor from his patio. He wondered what the night would bring. Hopefully not the usual. He was burned out on one-night stands and occasional flings with married women. Tonight he wanted the woman of his dreams—the very one he had spent ten years thinking about.

Early on in the day, he stopped at the Beverly Center to cop himself a suit from the Stacey Adams Collection, with shoes to match. After examining himself in the new three piece with pin stripes, he brushed a hand across the suede of his shoe before grabbing his keys and locking the door on his way outside.

The breeze blew across his face as he looked at the stars in the sky, which sat like diamonds. He inhaled the aroma of his neighbor's BBQ before jumping into his white BMW 750. As the Beemer came alive, the sounds of Donnell Jones blasted from the Bose system. He pressed to track number three as he skirted off heading to the 405

Freeway, with his dashboard clock reading ten minutes to eight.

* * *

About twenty minutes later, Heath pulled into the parking lot of the Hollywood Park Casino and made a phone call. When it picked up, the voice on the other end sounded excited to finally have gotten a call from a long-time friend whom he hadn't seen since the beginning of his incarceration. His voice was raspy, like rapper Ja Rules, when he answered.

"What's up, Heath? I'm inside with the kids at the blackjack table. Where you at?"

Iron'RE was a Canadian citizen who flew down every now and again to do business. He hadn't seen his friend Heath since his release from prison. The 750 and the condo were welcome-home gifts to show his appreciation for being on the team and staying stomped down by keeping his mouth shut.

Iron'RE ran a mafia lifestyle that ranged from Canada to as far as his home country of India. The "kids" was code for his foot soldiers, which was a clever way to throw off the Feds if they were tapped into any of their phone conversations.

The casino was packed like any other Saturday night. Cigarettes

3

and watered-down drinks were being passed around like prostitutes as the players sat at tables hoping to make it big.

Iron'RE got up from the table and placed the phone in his pocket while grabbing the icy drink that was being carried by a young lady who couldn't have been any older than the age limit required to drink in the state of California.

He met up with Heath at the front entrance, giving him an embrace that only a father would give to a son who he was proud of.

"Heath, my friend! It's been a minute. How you living'?" he asked, taking notice of how strong his boy was looking.

Since ten years had passed, Heath was looking like a straight monster, Iron'RE thought to himself.

"You still looking good, bro. A lot of push-ups, huh?"

"You know what's up, Iron'RE. Them bastards took the weights, so ya boy had to do something to keep these thangs right!" he explained while looking at his biceps that were practically busting through his suit jacket. "I miss those days we used to get crackin' on that iron though, and from the looks of it, I can see you been on ya game too!" he said, giving Iron'RE a squeeze on the arms with a soft-tone whistle

"So, you been out a year now, huh? Good to know you been keeping ya nose clean."

They began walked toward the entrance of the casino where it was less noisy. Three women walked in just as they were walking outside. They were dressed in short miniskirts and high heels while smoking cigarettes. It was obvious that they were prostitutes out to catch a vic (victim).

The two looked in admiration as the three hoochies waved and blew kisses.

"Come on, Heath! Not our taste tonight," Iron'RE said. "Tonight, we embark on a different territory."

He took his phone from his pocket and looked at the screen.

"I have this club I just bought into, and I wanted you to come with me to check it out. It's one of the reasons I came down," he said as he looked at Heath and grinned. "Besides, I haven't seen you in a decade, and I remember how much of a party animal you used to be."

Heath looked at his friend for a moment. He smiled at the memories he had played over and over in his head while in prison. It was just one of the tools he used that kept him from going crazy. But that wild life wasn't for him anymore. The club scene was getting

5

old, and he was ready to settle down.

"How's ya wife doing, bro?"

"She's been great. Just great. The doctor was able to cut away the knot she had on her breast from the implants. So now we're suing the idiot that did the operation for malpractice, but she's healthy though," Iron'RE said as he looked at Heath. "She told me to have you call sometime."

It felt strange to be talking about his wife's implants at a time like this. Iron'RE was ready for business.

"So you coming to the club?"

Heath looked at him with trepidation before answering.

"I'm kinda burnt out on the club scenes. I need to find that one, and we know that ain't crackin' at the club. Ain't no good broads there!"

"I told you, bro, that I just bought into this club. I wanna go check it out and make sure everything is straight. And I want you to come with me," Iron'RE said as they both headed back toward the entrance of the casino. "It's a lesbian club anyways. A club full of dykes and bisexuals, so you don't have to worry about finding that special one 'cause she won't be there!"

The last part took a minute to register.

"A lesbian club!" he said quietly to himself.

Heath knew that the game had taken a turn with the new millennium, but he never thought about a club for lesbians, dykes, bis, or whatever. This was something new as well as a good business move.

"What's the name of the club?"

Iron'RE looked up from his phone while his fingers continued to work the screen.

"It's called Catch One."

The club was just about twenty minutes away, just southwest of the casino. Iron'RE rolled into the car with Heath while the kids followed behind.

The 750 sped up Crenshaw Boulevard in the gutter lane. The weekends were what brought the street alive. Nice cars with big rims and beautiful women flossed up and down the boulevard with no particular place to go, but to simply hang out and hook up before the night's end.

Heath knew the business. Just as the girls were out, so were the jackers, and he was a victim himself coming up as a young baller. At

7

one point or another, everyone that was hood rich would experience being on the other side of the gun, with the barrel pointed at them and being told to come up off whatever they were on. And that's what had happened to him on this very boulevard, when he got jacked for his hot-ass '63 Chevy Impala in its wet paint that he had just picked up from Castro's Auto Paint Shop. It was cold how they did it, too. The broad just came out of nowhere.

"Hey, babes!" she called out before she began dancing on him with all that ass.

He was so distracted that he didn't see the clown coming up from behind him, who then smacked him in the back of the head with his pistol, leaving him unconscious or dead as his low-rider skirted out.

Although, later down the line, Heath did find out who had done it, and he handled the situation. He knew that he never wanted to get caught slipping like that again. So as he sped through traffic, his antennae were on point.

The scene was no different when they pulled up to the club. The lot was packed as music fell through opened windows. The aroma of cannabis lingered in the air while alcohol was being consumed through Styrofoam cups.

Some ladies moved through the parking lot dressed in jeans, button-downs, and Timberlands. They approached the car next to Heath's with two cuties inside, opened the door, and climbed inside. The driver who was dressed in a mini-jacket smiled as her intruder reached over for an embrace.

As Heath watched from the driver's seat, she stuck her tongue down her mouth.

"Yo, Iron'RE! Check this shit out!"

Iron'RE was distracted by his cell phone and lifted a finger for Heath to wait a minute while he continued to text.

When he was finished, he looked up and then stared through the passenger's window at the front door of the club. Heath nudged his shoulders while keeping his eyes on the young stud that was now sucking on the other girl's breast.

"Bro, you gotta get a look at this! What has the world come to?"

Heath was too busy looking at the action in the car next to him that he didn't notice the expression on his friend's face.

Iron'RE put a hand on his shoulder as he turned to look at him. "Let's go inside."

"What's the matter, bro?" Heath asked, when he suddenly

9

noticed the glare in his friend's eyes—the same glare he always had when it was time to take care of business. "I thought we were here to have some fun. I know that look, and it ain't cool!" he said, switching his position in the driver's seat. "That's the look when somebody stabbed you in the back."

He put one hand on the wheel and looked his friend in the eye. "Now, tell me. What kinda business do we have here?"

It was true that Iron'RE had every intention of having fun that night. He had come to the States to see his boy who he had not seen in quite a while and take him out for a night on the town. But he also had to tie up some loose ends on a business deal. When they arrived at the club, he was informed of some bad news.

"It seems that my business partner has just reneged on our arrangement," he explained to Heath while still looking at the front entrance of the club. "It was agreed upon to relinquish 80 percent of the club to me while he kept 20 percent in order to pay back a debt left undone in Canada."

"And now he's on the run?" Heath questioned.

"It appears so!"

"Well, just have the kids go lookin' for him and drag his ass back, Iron'RE."

"That's just it, bro. He was one of ours."

Heath put his second hand on the wheel and looked straight ahead. He looked in the rear-view mirror and saw that the two kids that followed them were being entertained by two young ladies who looked like they weren't into women at all. His hand came off the steering wheel, and he massaged his right temple.

"Who was it? Anybody I know?"

For a minute, Iron'RE took his eyes off the front entrance. He then looked back over at Heath, and his eyes began to water.

"What's up, bro? Who was it?" Heath asked, knowing that this shit was serious.

"It was Que! The boy clipped me in a major way!" he said, looking back at the club. "But the money is not important. It's the betrayal that hurts the most."

Heath couldn't believe what he was hearing right then. Not Que! Heath was the one who introduced Que to Iron'RE—the one that put him on.

It was Heath that had met Que after a squabble he had in front of Al's Liquor Store, which later turned into a shootout. Que was a total

11

stranger at the time, but he came to Heath's rescue with guns blazing.

After the smoke had cleared, Heath had found out that Que was a stock boy for the Iranian who owned the store. The owner was looking for some guns to buy in order to support the guerilla warfare that was taking place in his home country. And just like that, a few gun sales were made between the two for the Iranian man, and Heath and Que became the best of friends.

"What I need you to do is go inside. We both go in together, but we have to split up," he ordered Heath. "I haven't met her, but I'm pretty sure that Que has given her my description, so she will probably be alert."

"She? Who's she?"

"She is Que's niece."

He looked around to see where the kids were before continuing.

"Her name is Jai. She's been helping run the place. We were supposed to meet here tonight to go over the arrangements," Iron'RE began before he looked back at Heath. "I was keeping that on the hush. I wanted to surprise you. It would have been like old times with the three of us. But now he's gone!"

"How do you know this?"

Iron'RE showed him the text on his phone that was left by Que just minutes ago. He scrolled down the screen as he read: "Iron'RE, I know you all too well. There's no way you gonna allow me to live after what I have done. I gotta go while I have the chance."

Heath looked at the phone as he continued to scroll. He couldn't believe that Que would turn his back on Iron'RE like this. He treated him like a brother.

"What's up with ol' boy? Why he do some dumb shit like that and then put his niece in harm's way?"

"I have no intentions of harming women, Heath!" Iron'RE confirmed while stuffing his phone back into his pocket. "And he knows this, which is why he left her to run the club. And I'm also quite sure that he didn't inform her of his whereabouts. But I want to be positive."

Iron'RE then looked toward the front door of the club once again.

"I want you to get close to her and gain her trust, and see if she can convey any clues as to where he may be."

Heath looked out the driver's-side window and thought about his road dawg, and he reminisced for a minute about when times were good.

He knew the results when crossing Iron'RE, and so did Que. He wanted no more dealings with this life, but now that Que was involved, he knew that it wouldn't take much for Iron'RE to influence him. He looked once again though the rear-view mirror.

"Who are those two?"

Iron'RE walked up to the car and knocked on the passenger side window. His two bodyguards were in deep conversation with two cuties that looked like they were down for whatever. The one in the front seat of the SUV gave Iron'RE a look as if she didn't want to be bothered. But before the words could come out of her mouth, the passenger door flew open as a calm voice asked her to get lost. She looked at the figure before her that was cleanly dressed and shaven with his hand extended, and she found herself confused by the brute's courtesy that he was displaying.

The kids were told to stay in the car and keep surveillance. Que was well aware of Iron'RE's skills, and Iron'RE knew that he could just as well be sitting right under their noses, right in the parking lot.

The club was getting packed. Heath used the two cuties to get inside. Once inside, he found a table in the corner and sat one of the girls on his lap.

"So, what's ya name, baby girl?"

The young cutie was bouncing and gyrating in his lap to Lil Wayne's song "Lollipop" as she yelled into his ear.

"Well, check me out, Diamond! You and ya cousin go on and have a good time, and stay outta trouble!"

Heath then reached into his pocket and gave her a bill. "Here, drinks on me!"

The young girl then smiled and left with a peck on the cheek.

Heath made sure that he picked a table close to the bar, because he figured Jai would be coming out to check on the bartenders from the office. Now all he had to do was devise a plan that would get her attention.

About ten minutes had passed before Heath saw Iron'RE walk in the front entrance. He looked more for business and then pleasure as he stood in the doorway surveying the place.

His Armani suit was tailor-made, with the heels of its legs falling just above the Kenneth Coles that sported his feet. His short but stout frame drew attention from almost everyone that passed by, observing the unusual long braid that fell down the middle of his suit jacket. The lesbians rolled their eyes as they walked by, intimidated by a man who could wear a suit so well, while the bisexuals took mental notes, saving the image in their mental database. Iron'RE disregarded the glares and stares with only one mission in mind. He zeroed in on the back office. It was located just past the dance floor around the bar, with a sign on the door that read Employees Only.

His wide frame with big arms moved across the dance floor, past the gyrating flesh that was going crazy from the music that was being played by the DJ.

He made it to the door and knocked. There was a brief moment that he thought about just walking in, but he decided against it because he knew it would be the demise of his plan.

A voice from the other side of the door was soft but firm, and called to the stranger to come in.

As he entered, he stood in the doorway and casually looked

around and admired the exquisite taste of the gentleman he once called his brother. The office was no bigger than a two-car garage, but the choice of furniture made it look like a presidential suite.

Surveillance screens were mounted to the wall just above the doorway, monitoring all activity from the parking lot to the front door of the office. He smiled as he watched multiple screens go back and forth to the different images.

"Quite impressive," he said.

"How can I help you?" the young lady inquired, sitting at a black marble desk with her face glued to the computer screen as her fingers tapped along the keyboard.

"You may not want to be too close to the screen. You could lose your eyesight that way!" he warned, stepping inside and closing the door behind him.

The young lady looked up and threw her ponytail across her back.

"Excuse me, who are you?"

"Yes, indeed! Pardon my intrusion. My name is Amad. I'm a business associate of the club's owner, and was told that I should meet him here."

Iron'RE took a seat at the leather futon that sat against the wall across from her desk while unbuttoning his suit jacket and nearly exposing the butt of his gun.

The young lady reached for her glasses as she stood from her desk. She glanced at her security screen as she put them on.

"What did you say your name was again?"

"Amad. Amad Shafeef. I am an associate of Quency's. I was told to meet him here."

The young lady walked around to the mini-bar stationed alongside a back door that led to an easy exit though the back alley. One that Que may have been in and out of for the past week or so, Iron'RE surmised.

She reached into the cupboard to make sure that the pistol was exactly where her uncle had said it was in case of emergencies, and felt for the handle before grabbing a bottle of Remy Martin.

"My uncle hasn't been seen in the last two weeks," she replied with her back turned as she fixed herself a drink. "What type of business did you say you had with him?"

"I didn't. I merely said that I was an associate of his. You are his niece, you say?"

Iron'RE already knew this information as well as the fact that she was there to help run the club. But he played the game in order to get as much information as he could, so that he could locate the man who had stolen hundreds of thousands in American currency from him over a six-month period. And it was important that he found him fast.

"Yes, my name is Jai."

She walked back around the desk with the cup in one hand and extended the other for a handshake.

"I apologize for the untimely introduction. It's just that I've been so busy running this club, and I've been stressed that I have not heard from him. It's unlike him to go this long without contact."

Jai then offered him a drink, but he declined. She then sat back down to look at the computer, going through the last emails that she had received from Que, but none informed her of any meeting. But there was one notation that she quickly ran her eyes across before responding.

"I'm sorry. But I'm looking, and I don't see anything confirming your arrival."

"Well, that would be possible, since you haven't seen him in the past few weeks."

He crossed his legs as he studied an old Indian rug that he was certain he had given to Que as a gift. It was a priceless, handmade piece made in his homeland.

"He didn't say where he was going? Perhaps on a trip?"

"That's impossible. He would have called me," she said. "Anyway, I called his cell phone, but it kept going to voicemail. I also looked at his Facebook page and still got nothing."

Que was smart. He was obviously staying under the radar. No computer trail or nothing, he thought.

But then Iron'RE remembered his phone and the text that he had received from Que almost an hour ago. He was certain that he hadn't filled her in. Maybe he told her a strange reason for his absence, but informed her to tell no one. Whatever the case was, he thought that she was playing her part real cool.

* * *

The suit fit the businessman's profile, but he came in here with no briefcase or any type of material, saying that he was down for business, she thought. Besides, Jai knew that anyone from a drug lord to the Feds could be looking for her uncle.

She also saw the butt of the gun as Iron'RE studied the rug. The shift on the futon had exposed his waist, allowing the black Beretta to peek through his jacket, which made her nervous.

She got up from her desk and walked back over to the bar to grab the .380 caliber that was now exposed with the barrel pointed at Iron'RE.

The swift move was of no surprise. In fact, Iron'RE smiled at her bravado as he stood to his feet calmly.

"I take it that this meeting has taken an unfortunate turn, my darling. What's with the firearm?"

She stood there, not knowing what to do. Her had uncle taught her how to use a weapon when she was a kid, even taking her to the shooting range. But never had she been confronted with a real-life situation like this.

Although she was the niece of a gangster, her reality was the life of a princess. And now there was a total stranger in her office with a gun down his pants asking questions about someone that she loved so dearly.

"What type of business do you have with Que, huh? You better start talking, or I'm gonna think that you were here to rob me, and

I'll put a bullet right between your eyes."

Iron'RE sat back down on the futon just as poised as he when he had entered. He buttoned up his coat to conceal his weapon, and assured her that he had no plans on using it.

"You must relax. I have told you that your uncle and I had some matters to discuss about future plans. Some that I wish not to disclose." He pointed to his gun. "I assure you there's no problem at all. I also am a business man and carry for protection. I'm sorry to have alarmed you."

Iron'RE got up slowly from where he sat, but Jai wasn't taking any chances. She kept the pistol lined up with his forehead as she moved back to her desk.

"Well, like I said, I haven't seen him in a while now. But if I do, I'll let him know that you came by. Amad, is it?"

She pushed a button under her desk, and within seconds two heavy-set men appeared. Their T-shirts hugged their biceps, with the word Security on the back.

"Please escort this gentleman out, will you?"

The two muscled men began to escort Iron'RE as ordered through the door of the office, until she protested.

"No! Take him through the back exit, please. I don't want to cause any distractions for business."

She then set the gun on the desk as the men led him through the exit.

"And, Amad, once again, if I hear from him, I will relay the message."

"Don't bother, flower. I guess that I will have to resort to other measures," he explained as he disappeared through the exit.

Once he got outside and into the parking lot, he jumped in the car where the kids stood watch. He was certain that she was watching from the surveillance setup that she had in her office. So he decided to drive up to the service station, where he got in touch with Heath.

This girl was clever, he thought. She was playing the role all too well, and was probably calling Que right then to let him know that he had come by looking for him. He then shot Heath a text to give him a heads-up.

Heath was at the bar sitting next to a Da Brat lookalike and a red-haired Asian girl. They were talking about some chapters from the *Fifty Shades of Grey* book, when he saw the two bouncers go through the office door.

After ten minutes had passed, when neither one of them emerged, Heath became worried. He was just about to go to the back of the room, when he got a hit on his cell phone.

He sat back down at the bar to read the text, while the two women played with each other's lips.

He looked at the two having fun together, hoping to be a third party before the night was through, before he turned toward the screen to read the text:

Heath, I think the girl knows that we're looking for him. She has the whole place, including the parking lot, under surveillance. There's a back door in the office that leads to the parking lot. She had two goons escort me out that way. Didn't want to take a chance by your car, so me and the kids are at the gas station up the street. And PS, the bitch pulled a gun on me. PPS, All smiles.

Heath smiled once he finished reading the text.

"Can I get a double shot of Hennessy?"

* * *

Jai sat at her desk and poured herself another shot of Remy Martin. She took a sip and set the glass down next to the pistol.

Her ponytail was now untwisted, hanging over her shoulders

24

while running down the spine of her back, exposing her beauty while under pressure. Her jet-black hair was essential to the milky skin she owned.

She was a sexy red-bone, who had been raised in Inglewood, California. Her mother allowed her to live with her uncle, because the streets were too rough in her hometown of Oakland.

Jai was Irish and Black, and it showed, from her beautiful complexion to the structure of her cheek bones. She was famously complimented with the resemblance of Alicia Keys every time she went out to the clubs, where she soon became a highly accepted regular. Once she had found out that the club was for sale, she notified her uncle and told him that it would be a smart investment, and that she could help him run it. With her notoriety and out-of-the-closest bisexuality, she was certain that she could bring in more business.

She set her glass back down and pulled out her iPhone. Her fingers trembled as she scrolled to her contacts, where she stopped at her uncle's name. She paused for a minute, trying to remember the description of the man who had just left her office.

"You can't miss him. He has a long braid running down his

back," her uncle had warned her.

Her fingers moved quickly over the screen of her phone as she texted the message that would bring her uncle to a natural dread. In all capital letters she began to text:

"THE MAN WITH THE MONGOLIAN STOPPED BY!"

Seconds later, her phone rang. She got up from her desk, walked across the room, locked the door, and sunk into the futon before answering.

Her uncle's voice was calm as it came through the other end, and she couldn't understand why. Here it was, this man, a total stranger to her, had come into her office dressed like the mafia, toting a gun in his waist while inquiring about her uncle's whereabouts, and yet her uncle was so calm. She wasn't buying that story about him being a businessman either. He better start explaining to her quickly, she thought.

"Yes, he showed up in my office asking about you," she began. "You told me to call you if anybody came in with that description, but you never told me that he would bring a gun! Que, what kinda trouble did you get into?"

She held her forehead in the palm of her hand as her hair draped forward, obscuring the nervous look on her face. Her uncle reassured her that everything would be okay and not to worry. He knew that he would never show again.

Heath sat at the bar playing with the corner of his Hennessy while the Asian gal nibbled pieces of ice cubes on "Da Brat's" earlobe. Her body gyrated to the sounds of The Dream's single titled "I Love Ya Girl" as her hand played the piano up her thigh.

They were both bisexual, so neither objected when Heath came over and stuck his tongue down the Asian's mouth. "Da Brat" followed suit by putting her hand down his leg where his phallus sat stiff as she started kissing him on his neck. The Asian girl moaned beneath the sounds of the music while she was feeling herself. He grabbed her by the hand and headed for the door.

"What's ya name, baby girl?" he asked as he opened up the door to his 750.

"Ohhh, is this ya Beemer? This shit is tight!" "Da Brat" said. "Her name is Octavia and I'm Kayla."

* * *

The mornings were never again like the ones when he woke up in prison. While incarcerated, he woke up to the sounds of locks and slamming doors, with another man on the top bunk waiting to jump down to use the toilet. Not this morning. This morning, like many others since he had gotten out of prison, he was sleeping on satin sheets and wearing silk pajamas while waking up to soft flesh with a beautiful fragrance.

He reached over and grabbed the breasts of Octavia, which were exposed as she lay on her back. They sat firm on her chest like two coffee cups with nipples between the perfect line of her torso. She had a petite body in her five-foot frame, which confirmed her Asian heritage. His hands couldn't resist the camel toe that protruded from the crease of her boy shorts that she wore beneath her jeans that were now on the floor.

The touch brought her to life as her eyes opened while her hand joined his, bringing her hips to gyrate. The toilet flushed from the bathroom as the door swung open, and a naked Kayla came to the foot of the bed with unspoken agreement, pulling her friend's shorts off and onto the floor.

Heath fired up a blunt while the three of them lay on the bed watching the flat-screen that was plastered to the wall above the bar set.

So far, everything had gone according to plan. After finding out that the two were old friends of Jai's, Heath saw no reason to stick around. All he needed to know, he would get from these two hoochies soon enough.

The smoke from the cannabis climbed to the ceiling as Heath exhaled. As Octavia looked up, he grabbed her mouth firmly and gave her a charge. Her vagina throbbed as the hemp began to take its effect.

He looked at Kayla, who reached for the blunt.

"What flava is this, daddy?" she asked as he passed it over to her without responding.

Suddenly, he thought about the freaky things that crossed his mind while in prison, and decided this would be the perfect time to see if they worked.

Heath went into the kitchen to retrieve the turkey baster and the white illegal substance that he kept in a little box. When he returned to the room, the girls saw what was in his hands and smiled.

* * *

"How'd it go the other night?"

Iron'RE was decked out in his Armani suit and suspenders, with his Mongolian freshly braided and running down his back. He blended in perfectly at the ESPN Zone near the Staples Center, where he and his good friend had decided to meet for breakfast.

Iron'RE picked a quiet corner next to the big screen that was displaying footage of the Mayweather and Sugar Shane Mosley bout. All bets were on Mosley for the first couple of rounds, especially when he caught Money Mayweather across the chin with that right hook. But that just woke up the beast as Mayweather snapped out of it . . . and that was all she wrote.

"When I saw them two goons go back there, I knew something was up. I started to slide back there with my pistol out, until I got the text," Heath said as he took a bite from the stack of waffles.

He then glanced back at the screen. An ad was playing, announcing that the Lakers were to battle the Phoenix Suns on Thursday night at the Staples Center.

The place was packed, and Heath could have sworn he had seen the beautiful Lynn Toler, the star judge from *Divorce Court*, walk in. After having a thought, he looked back down at his plate of waffles and returned to the subject before taking another bite.

"She pulled a gun on ya, huh?" The waffle filled his mouth as he chewed on both sides. "What was it, a .22? A .9?"

"The bitch had a .380!" Iron'RE said. "I could tell that she wasn't accustomed to it either, 'cause her hand was slightly shaking."

"Slight shaking, huh? That's a cold son of a bitch, Iron'RE, to put his people in the mix like this. I didn't think Que would get down like that!" Heath continued as he swallowed the last of his breakfast.

He took a swig of his mango juice and then wiped off his mouth with a napkin before reaching into his pocket for a Newport. He was reaching for his lighter when he noticed the No Smoking sign and set the pack back on the table.

"I thought you quit!"

"I did, but after the episode the other night, I must have fallen back on old habits."

He then reached for his phone and showed Iron'RE some pictures.

"This is Octavia and Kayla, both are bisexual. And, bro, they some freaks!"

As Iron'RE looked at the pics, he continued. "These two broads are friends with the niece. What's her name, Jai?" he said, hoping he got the name right. "Well, anyway, they said they went to school together and see her all the time at the club."

Iron'RE was never one to get excited. He continued to look at the pictures.

"Did they tell you her place of residence?" he asked.

"Que got her a place on Washington and La Brea down by the Comedy Union. They having brunch this week for her birthday at Rosco's Chicken & Waffles down the street from there."

"Did they say anything about Que?"

Heath shook his head.

"I didn't wanna say too much 'bout him yet. Besides, I was too busy with the turkey baster!"

Iron'RE gave it thought before shaking his head, and decided to leave it alone.

"That penitentiary turned you into a monster!" he joked.

CHAPTER THREE

Reckless

A few months ago, you couldn't have paid Jai to leave the house without her hair and makeup being done. Even if she was just going to the local department store, she just had to leave the curling iron on hot. But today she rushed out the house in just her sweatpants and hoodie, sporting some pink Chuck Taylors on her feet.

Her cell phone was pressed to her ear as she jumped into her car, a special gift from her uncle for her eighteenth birthday.

And what better way to complement her achievements than to buy her an S-class 550 Mercedes Benz?

Three years later and the car still looked as if it was just shipped from the country that made it.

It never made a sound as it came alive, moving like a stealth when she backed out of her driveway and down the street into traffic.

She bobbed and weaved through the less fortunate automobiles like an irresponsible kid who had just taken her parents' car without permission. Every corner she hit was precise though, and from the eyes of an experienced driver, one would say that she had skills.

Her phone was still glued to her ear when she switched lanes in total disregard to the violation of operating a vehicle while using a handheld device.

She stopped at a red light as a car pulled up beside her. The young man stared at her with the sounds banging from his truck, obviously struck by her beauty. He nodded at the light and then back at her. It was obvious that he wanted to see if the 550 was overrated.

She smiled as the light turned green, and smashed the accelerator. The 550 sped off with the Cadillac in hot pursuit, reaching speeds up to 75 MPH in a 35 MPH zone. Jai's jaw dropped when she saw that the Cadillac was on the side of her, with the driver watching her instead of the road.

She nodded for him to look ahead as she slowed down, but it was too late. The two of them came to a red light, and the Cadillac blew through the intersection. He never knew what hit him. The truck coming from the other direction smacked dead into the passenger side, sending the car airborne.

The light turned green as Jai drove away, shaking her head.

"That's a cold-hearted broad," Heath said under his breath as he drove slowly through the intersection, looking at the damage from the accident which unfolded right before his eyes.

Heath knew that something like this could happen the way she was driving. From the time he left her house until now, Jai had been driving like a ghost. If it wasn't for the device he attached to her car the night before, he would have had no chance of keeping up with her. But he had to admit that she had skills, and he thought she would have been a good getaway driver back in his days of robbing banks. Besides, she was kind of fly, too.

She had a swag about herself that he began to find intriguing. The way she left the house in her hoodie and pink Chucks made the blood rush to his head. And when Iron'RE told him that she had pulled a gun on him, the heat really turned up in his loins.

"Man, this broad is crazy! But I'm diggin' her in a real way."

Heath sat in his car as Jai pulled up to the salon at Leimert Park. He watched as she got out of her car with her phone still glued to her ear as she went inside.

"Hey, Ruthy B, I hope I'm not late."

She went straight for the empty chair without signing in and set her purse down on the table.

Ruthy B stared at her with a motherly, loving smile. She was short and stubby with a scarf wrapped around her head Aunt Jemima style, and skin as tough as nails.

Ruthy B was the oldest stylist in the salon, with the soul of Mother Teresa. She kept the balance inside the salon. Customers both old and new came to love her because they could tell her anything and she'd always have an answer.

"I know you just didn't rush to get here, did you?" Ruth B said as she stared from Jai's hoodie to her sweats to her shoes. "Cute shoes though!"

Ruth B then took off the hoodie while her fingers went to work.

"You know you shouldn't be driving like that. Didn't you just get your license back? And, girl, you know it's all kind of crazy people out there just jumpin' into traffic like they got no business."

Jai gave her a pat on the hand while turning around.

"I know, Ruthy B, but I was trying to make my appointment so that I could get my hair done for my birthday."

Ruthy B stopped groping and dropped her hands to her sides.

"Well, I must be getting old. How could I forget that?" she said. "For the last five years, I've been doin' your hair, girl. I neva forgot.

Ya mean to tell me that today is May the 30th?"

She then looked at the calendar above her, pointing at the date with her comb.

"Well, I'll be damned. Happy birthday, girl! How old you is today?" she asked Jai after giving her a big hug.

The ladies in the nearby stations greeted her with a wave while wishing her the same.

After telling Ruthy B that she had turned twenty-three, Jai reclined in the chair as the comb went to work. As she relaxed while sitting in the chair, she thought about this day last year.

Ricco was sitting in the waiting area while she got beautified up for a special night on the town. They had plans to drive to Las Vegas that night for her birthday to enjoy a romantic night under the stars and bright lights. But the more they spent the day together, the more arguments they got into.

Ricco had been her first love. The two had been together ever since she graduated from high school. At times, he could be the sweetest man ever, but when he got around his boys, his whole attitude would change. He became abusive and accused her of cheating, and it was beginning to get a little played out.

37

That night she decided that enough was enough, and she would tell him that it was over once they returned from Vegas. But she waited up that night crying her pretty little eyes out because he didn't show up. She was thinking that Ricco had trashed her night on purpose, until she got the call from Octavia telling her that her man had just been killed. Octavia saw Ricco leave Fred's Liquor Store and heard what sounded like backfire from a car as the wheels screeched away from the scene. When she saw that it was Ricco lying on the ground with pieces of his head missing, there was nothing that she could do but call her homegirl to give her the news.

A year had passed since the tragedy, but every time that she was at the salon, she was reminded of that unfortunate night.

"Are you okay, sweetie?" Ruthy B asked as she gave Jai a squeeze on her shoulder while she continued running the comb through her hair.

She knew that every time Jai sat in her chair, there was always that moment tugging at her.

"I think it's time that you let the past stay where it's at," she suggested.

But what Ruthy B didn't know was that just as soon as Jai

walked out the doors, those moments of Ricco would vanish. Tonight she was going to the Catch One, but not as the manager. Tonight she was going to be VIP and celebrate her birthday with her newfound friend, Charline (a.k.a. Blac Chyna).

"You right, Ms. Ruthy. Today I gotta let the past stay where it's at, and let tonight write my new beginnings," she announced as she came out from her daze.

"That's the spirit, sweetie," she exclaimed as she handed her a mirror. "Here ya go. Take a look!"

Heath waited in the car outside the salon as the morning began to take its transformation into a blissful afternoon. The clouds dissipated and exposed the sun as the heat showed its mercy on visitors enjoying the day in front of stores with a nice game of chess.

Two hours had passed as he patiently waited before the 550 once again came alive. He remembered the tracking device and decided not to tail her this time.

The 750 pulled up on the side of her at a red light. Only this time she was the one that looked inside. She smiled at the driver, who nodded slightly as she hit the accelerator when the light turned green.

Heath wanted to roll down the window to let her know how lucky her man was to wake up to her every morning, but it was too early in the game for that. He knew that he had to stick to the script for the sake of loyalty to his friend, Iron'RE.

Just as he thought, she pulled into the parking lot of the packed establishment. It was a busy afternoon by the sight of the long line of customers running along the sidewalk all waiting to get inside to eat lunch.

Kayla and Octavia were already inside. Heath noticed that once Jai got out of her car and went straight for the door, she still had her phone glued to her ear.

Heath pulled into the parking lot as the valet rushed over to his car and signaled for him to stop. There was nowhere to park. The plump little man tapped on his window to give him the unfortunate news.

The young valet driver wore a bootleg T-shit with the face of Michael Jackson plastered on the front. It was a knock-off of the original Michael with the '80s Jheri curl that caught on fire in the Pepsi commercial. He also had on a vest missing three buttons that looked like it was picked from the rack of a thrift store.

Beads of sweat trickled down the fat man's face as the white glove went to retrieve them.

"You can't park nowhere, bro!" he said to Heath as he swept the other gloved hand around with an all-Irie look on his face.

Heath paid him no attention. He knew that he was probably the neighborhood crack monster getting paid under the table to keep the parking lot tight.

"A'right, big dawg. No sweat! I'll just park around the corner," Heath called out as he drove off.

The place was packed when Jai walked inside. Octavia and Kayla were happy to see the birthday girl as she sat down at the table. They picked a spot near the corner next to a nice-sized window that was tinted from the outside to block the sun. It was cool for Jai, because she wanted to keep an eye on her car. When she looked out the window, she saw the 750, the one she was next to at the light with the handsome man inside.

"I just saw that guy a few blocks ago," she said.

"Girl, who?" Octavia swung around to look.

"Right there. In that white Beemer!"

"Nice ride!" Kayla said, even though neither of the girls could see the driver who had just spent the night with the both of them a couple days before.

"Girl, he was fine, too! I thought he was going to roll down his window, but the light turned green," Jai added.

"What's up with tonight, bitch? Are we at the Catch or what?" Octavia asked, no longer wanting to talk about the guy in the 750.

For a long time now, she had a crush on her girl, Jai, but she never told her the business.

"Yeah, you on tonight or are you playing with the game?" Kayla questioned, looking up to help the waitress with the food.

Jai ordered her favorite just before she had arrived, which was chicken and waffles.

"Why thank you!" the red-headed server said while while setting down the food in front of them.

She was tall and slim and in her early twenties, with the body of a beach volleyball player. The name on her tag read Taliah. She had mahogany skin and hazel eyes, and she had the cheek bones that made her look Egyptian.

"You don't have to play cordial, mamma. These are my girls from another world, Jai and Octavia," Kayla said. "Today is my girl Jai's birthday, and we came to celebrate with a little brunch."

"Well, happy birthday, Jai. Hope that it's beautiful for you today!" Taliah said with a smile as she looked over at Kayla. "See you later."

"Don't tell me you hittin' that, girl!"

"Nah, but I'm working on it!" she said, before wishing her girl a happy birthday again. "So are we on tonight?"

Just as Jai was about to respond, her phone rang. Her uncle was on the other line calling from the office while going over the surveillance tapes from the other night. She knew what he was doing because she could hear the ping from the computer as he pressed on the keys.

"Where you at, Unc? In the office?" she asked while pulling skin from the chicken with her phone wedged between her chin and earlobe.

On the other end, Que smiled while his niece continued to talk with a mouth full of food. She had been this way ever since he knew her, and no birthday would ever change that.

"Yes, I'm here. Happy birthday, sweetheart."

He began to tell her about the gift he had gotten her, but stopped when he heard a noise coming from the back. The monitor was busy sending the feed to the computer from last week's footage. But it didn't catch the image of a person in the back alley dressed in black. He hit a few keys on the board, and the screen suddenly flashed to the back outside entrance.

"Jai, something's come up. Let me get back with you."

"Is everything okay? What's the matter?"

He paid no attention to her rhetorical question nor the alarm of her voice.

"Que, is everything all right? Why are you speaking so low?"

The phone went dead before she got an answer.

When she pulled up to the club, the parking lot was empty. She drove around the back to see if she could spot her uncle's car, but still nothing. Jai put the car in park and then dialed his number.

The call went straight to voicemail. She cursed to herself as she began to dial the number again.

"Come on, Que. Where are you?" she said to herself, hitting the steering wheel with the fists of both hands as the phone fell into her lap.

She looked around the vacant lot for any signs of her uncle, but came up short.

With her head lying back on the headrest, her fingers began to massage the left side of her temple, allowing her eyes to rest for a minute so that she could figure out her next move.

Jai thought about the last scare that Que had given her when he failed to return her call. He was away in Canada for business, but he was supposed to have been back to attend her eighteenth birthday party. Already an hour late, she had continued to blow up his phone and spent the day in worry. But she was relieved when a car pulled up wrapped in a big bow with a sign that read Happy Birthday, Jai!

She smiled at the memory of how surprising her uncle could be when he wanted to, and she wished that he would surprise her right then with a returned call so she would know he was all right.

A few minutes had passed when she opened her eyes to someone standing next to her car. It was the man at the light, she thought to herself. The one in the 750. Her startled face turned into a smile.

She blushed at her own thoughts as she stared at his lips, which sat gracefully inside a perfectly-trimmed goatee.

When he spoke, she couldn't hear because her thoughts were saturated with mental visions of what those lips could do to her.

It took a minute before she snapped out of it, and she immediately thought about how her uncle might be in danger. She looked down at her phone and then back at the man who stood at her window.

"Excuse me, miss. Is everything all right with you?"

He stood there wearing a white linen suit and gators, with his cell phone in hand ready to make a call for help if need be.

"I'm sorry, but have you been following me?"

Jai believed in coincidences, but she knew that there had to be a reason why she saw this man at the light and now here, especially at a moment like this.

"Do I know you? Why are you in front of my club?"

"Easy, sweetheart. What's up with all the questions? I'm just trying to make sure you're okay," he said as he stepped away from the car with both hands in the air like a felon that just got caught in the act.

"My name is Heath. No sweat, baby girl! I was just passing through and thought it would be a disservice if I was to just pass by without checking up on you. I mean ya had your head down and all."

She was checking him out for a minute, peeping out his swag before she responded.

"I'm sorry. Excuse me for being so rude. I just got a lot on my plate right now," she said, looking down at her phone before lifting her head back up at Heath.

When she returned her gaze, she found Heath looking at the front of the club.

"So, is this your club?"

"You know about the Catch?" she sounded surprised, not knowing why though because everyone knew about Catch One. "My uncle actually owns the club. I just help run it when he's away."

"Away? What you mean? Like he's in prison?"

She almost missed the humor until she saw the smile creep into the corner of his mouth.

"That was cute! What did you say your name was again?"

Heath extended his hand through the slightly rolled down window before she gave thought to roll it all the way down with the touch of a button.

"My name is Heath," he introduced himself as he grabbed her hand and held it.

She left it there, enjoying the warmth and strength it gave. For a minute, she almost forgot the reason she was there, until her phone rang again. She pulled her hand back and pressed the Accept button to answer. Heath stood there as her lips began to move while the window rolled up.

A minute had passed before she rolled it back down again to apologize.

"I'm sorry, my name is Jai. But, look, I gotta go right now," she explained, obviously in a hurry. "But thank you for checking up on me. You should stop by the club sometime."

"I'm not much of a clubgoer," he lied. "But tell ya what," he began as he reached into his pocket and pulled out a business card. "Here! Give me a call when you want a lil' service."

As she read the card, she now understood the reason for those nice firm hands of his.

"Massage, huh? You got your own massage business. That's what's up! I could use one of those one day," she said with a smile.

"Open twenty-four hours a day," he said while jumping into his car.

She smiled again as she pulled off.

* * *

He knew that she had received a call from Que, and that he might have been there just before they arrived, which is how she ended up here in the first place, he thought. Heath looked at the front door of the club as the 550 sped off into traffic. Putting his car in drive, he made a call to Iron'RE.

"What's up, bro?"

"I just got through talking to the niece. I followed her to the club."

"Was she able to tell you anything?"

"Not much yet, but she got a call while we were talking and suddenly had to go."

Heath was making his way around the back when he saw something next to a green trash bin. He jumped out of his car to look around while touching the butt of his pistol that was in the small of his back.

"Heath, what's up, bro? You still there?"

"One sec, bro!" He paused for a minute before answering again. "Iron'RE, there's something behind this bin."

He reached to push the bin aside. The body was slumped between the bin and the wall just outside the back of the club. The body's head fell back when Heath moved it, revealing the bullet wound between the eyes,

"Iron'RE, you still there? It's Monte. Looks like Que caught him slippin'."

"Is it bad?"

"Real bad, bro. One shot to the face," Heath informed him.

As Iron'RE spoke through the phone, Heath listened while

looking around to make sure that he was still alone.

After ending the call with his friend, Heath opened the passenger side of his car to set Monte inside, but not before covering his face to break the lens of the camera. Once inside his car, he drove the speed limit all the way to Belmont Shores, where he met up with Iron'RE and two of the kids so that they could dispose of the body.

f you watched TMZ and saw Rapper Tyga and Blac Chyna hand in hand on *Rendezvous* then you would know that she had body. And it was evident that spotting that big booty from around the corner wasn't hard to do at all. This is why Jai pulled into the parking lot of the Slavson Swap Meet when she saw her friend with the same name going inside.

The parking lot was packed as always with shiny rims and booming sounds pounding from trucks of low-riders and high-signers, giving the lot an aura of ghetto kings and queens.

Once she found a place to park, she jumped out and gave a donation to a well-shaved young Muslim who stood at the doorway soliciting newspapers and bean pies. She handed him a $20, and as he put it in his pocket, he handed her a paper, which she declined.

When she went inside, she immediately spotted her friend Blac Chyna bent over by the shoe store, trying on a pair of boots with her ass facing the aisle.

"Hey, girl!" she called while grabbing a handful.

"Bitch, what's good?" she hollered back.

Blac Chyna was well described, with an ass so fat you could see it even if it was hidden. Her real name was Charline. The real Blac Chyna just made her hood famous because she looked dead-on like her.

"Ya bash still on tonight?"

"Of course it is. That's why I came into this crowded-ass place. I spotted that big ass of yours going through them doors and wanted to let you know it was still crackin'!"

"Happy birthday, girl. Ya know I'm gonna be there. Just had to get these fly-ass boots," she replied while looking down at her feet. "You know I gotta come through grandstanding, girl!"

"I can dig it! So we still on after the party? Me and you?"

"Jai, you know I can't wait to take ya fine ass down tonight!" she said, giving her earlobe a taste with her tongue.

"Ohh, all right, baby girl. See you tonight then!" Jai answered, giving her one last squeeze before leaving.

Once she got back to her car, she looked down at her cell phone to check the time. She hadn't realized how much time had escaped her morning, since it was now almost 4:00 p.m. She pulled out of the parking lot and headed up Western Boulevard to make one last stop before heading home, so that she could get ready for her birthday bash.

Back at the swap meet, Blac Chyna was still bent over when she felt her ass being slapped again.

"Damn, Jai! What you doing, girl?"

"Who the hell is Jai? Was it that broad you just got through hollering at?" said a familiar voice.

Chub was a heavy-set Creo with a shiny bald head and goatee, and was dressed in his fresh Pro-Club T-shirt and Jabo Jeans. He was a regular around the swap meet, and all the Asians had grown to love him, because when he spent his cash, he bought enough gear to last him months. His paper was long, and he continued to stack, collecting from the many trap houses he had throughout LA and Compton.

He pulled out a wad of cash and handed the cashier two bills to cover his friend's expenses.

"What up, baby girl? See you still straddling the fence, huh?" he said as he grabbed her from behind, pressing hard against her, and whispered in her ear. "You know she can't do you like daddy can.

You betta stop playin' and holla at ya boy!" he said before turning to leave.

* * *

Men at Work was still open when Jai pulled into the establishment, which was an auto detailing shop that sold rims and beat for the trunks. When she pulled up, she spotted her uncle's car.

"I knew you would be here!" she said aloud.

Men at Work was a spot that her uncle had brought her to a while back. It gave the youngsters around the neighborhood jobs in order to keep them away from the gangs and drugs. Since she was a teen, Jai watched as this operation worked to her uncle's advantage, spreading his good deeds throughout the local police department. It had further received honors by the local police chief and Congresswoman Maxine Waters.

Once she got inside, she witnessed the hard work from the young man wearing brown khakis and holding a spray bottle and rags. He was wiping down the top-of-the-line vehicles, including Phantoms and Teslas.

She spotted Rodman behind the counter helping some customers select the proper dash (radio) for their ride.

"Hey, Rod, you see my uncle?" she called out as he was finishing up with them.

Rodman stood about six feet tall and towered over the customers as he helped them. He was born in Trinidad, and despite the twenty years he spent in the States, his accent was still thick. He used this to his advantage when it came to the female customers, who went crazy when he spoke. With his dark complexion and naturally curly hair, he smiled at the customers as he gave them their receipt.

"Thank you, and please come again."

He looked over at Jai and came around the counter to embrace her.

"What's up, Jai? How you been?"

"Not too good. Have you seen Que?"

"Not since last week. Why, what's up?"

"Why is his car here then?"

"Oh, he let me use it. Straight hoe busser, too."

"I'm sure it is," she said, breaking from his embrace. "Well, tell him to call me the next time you hear from him," she asked as she turned around. "Oh, you know it's gonna be poppin' tonight at the club. You there?"

"All the time, boo. Ya girl Octavia gonna be there?"

"You know she is. See you there!" she said as she walked out the door.

It was late in the evening when she pulled into the driveway of her home. She took a few minutes to herself as she sat in the driver's seat contemplating as to how her day had gone. Tonight was going to be one of the biggest bashes that she could ever throw for herself. All of her homegirls were going to be there—as would be her two road dawgz, Octavia and Kayla. And she also knew that Blac Chyna confirmed that she would stop by too, after seeing her earlier in the day.

She knew Blac Chyna had been waiting to take her down, and she had no problem in showing it every time they saw each other. At first, it was just a cat-and-mouse game. Every time Blac Chyna would come to the club, she would chase and Jai would run. She didn't know why though. Blac Chyna was fine as hell. But it wasn't until her birthday that she decided to give in and hit her up asking if they could hook up after the party. And Blac Chyna accepted.

After getting out of her car, she let the door close as she stood there looking at her reflection from the driver's side window. Her hair was fly, she thought as the Shirley Temples spilled out from the base of her hoodie.

Once she got inside, she went straight to the bathroom to draw a bath. After taking off her clothes, she jumped in and began to soak while thinking about the guy she met earlier that day.

CHAPTER SIX

RIP Monte

The ocean was dark and calm as the moonlight reflected upon it. It was a nice night out for any romantic couple that wanted to sail down lover's lane. But luckily for Heath and his team, there was not a soul in sight as they arrived at the docks.

They carried Monte's lifeless body as if they were carrying a drunken friend, just in case someone was nearby to see them and grow suspicious. He was every bit of 250 pounds of lean, pure muscle, yet they carried him with ease. When they got to the speed boat, Heath placed him into the passenger seat while Iron'RE started up the engine.

"You two go back to the car and wait for my call," he said to two of the kids as Heath untied the rope and jumped into the back of the boat. "Cover our tracks on the way to make sure we weren't spotted," he added as the boat wisped away like a phantom disappearing into the dark sea.

Once they got about two miles from shore, Iron'RE killed the switch and sat as the waves rocked the boat back and forth.

Taking a moment of silence, the two watched the sky, admiring what both of them had missed just minutes before. The stars were out gleaming in the sky like the black sand from an hourglass.

Heath reminisced on the brief encounter with Jai, and the sadness she displayed when he pulled up and how he was able to put a smile on her face with his charming words. He had been following her for the past few days now, and found himself beginning to take a liking to her. She had swag about her that he found different from the other chicks he dated. He could tell just from talking to her that she had the soul of a woman twice her age.

But now he was conflicted. Looking over at Iron'RE, he knew where his loyalty lay, and he knew that he could never cross his friend by mixing business with pleasure. So as they continued to float, he took hold of the corpse and threw it overboard.

"Rest in peace, Monte. We shall avenge your blood!" Iron'RE promised.

They both sat there for a minute not saying a word as Monte slowly descended into the sea.

The inside of the club was packed. The music was blaring, and 50 Cent's single "Just a Lil' Bit" had everyone on the dance floor gyrating with their hands in the air.

Jai watched from the surveillance cameras as her road dawgz made their entrance and headed straight for the VIP section to greet the birthday girl.

Everything was looking good. Her uncle paid for YG to perform that night, which she thought was cool. She had a long-time crush on YG and his thug mentality, and always wondered what it would feel like to embrace some of his thug passion.

When she got up the stairs to the VIP section, the DJ threw her a shout-out over the mic that got the whole building popping with cheers of celebration for the birthday girl, who the entire crowd had grown to know and love. Tonight was her night, and she was feeling good.

Octavia had invited some strippers from the neighborhood strip club, Starz, to shake some ass in the face of the birthday girl, and she enjoyed every bit of it. She slapped asses with her one hand while downing a glass of champagne with the other.

Feeling herself, Jai jumped up to bust open a fresh bottle, letting the bubbles fly.

"All right! Y'all bitches turn this shit up!" she yelled as the DJ took over, slapping on Lil John's hit single "Turned Down for What?"

Booty was popping all over the place as girls danced with each other while the guys speculated and waited to see which ones they could pull for a threesome.

It was approaching one o'clock in the morning, and Blac Chyna was still a no-show. Jai was now sitting in the booth with Octavia and Kayla.

"Girl, wasn't Blac Chyna supposed to be here? What's up with that?" Kayla questioned.

"Girl, I don't know. I saw her earlier at the Slavson. She said she was gonna make it, but I ain't gonna hold my breath," she said over the loud music.

"Oh, girl! Look! Ain't that YG!" Octavia called as the music stopped.

His hit single "My Hittas" began to take over. But before he performed, he gave a gangsta shout to the birthday girl and started spitting the bars through the mic.

* * *

"Oh, boy! Why you doing this to me? You know I'm supposed to be at Jai's birthday party. Oh, stop!" Blac Chyna lay on her stomach asshole-naked, looking back at Chub while his head was buried in her ass cheeks. "Oh, Chub. Please stop!" she pleaded again as her cheeks clapped to the tunes that played over the radio in his room.

"I told you that Jai can't serve you like this, coochie! Good girl, what planet you say you got this from?"

With one smooth motion, he pulled her up from the waist, sliding his pillow beneath her stomach, before he slid between her cheeks, smiling as they jiggled with every thrust of his hips.

"This shit is mine, baby girl. Not Jai's or nobody else's. You hear me?" he ordered her with a smile.

"Yes, daddy! Yes, daddy! I hear you, baby. This is yours. Ohhh! You got it, baby. You got it!" she moaned.

It was going to be a promising day, she thought as the sun was raised, giving life to the beautiful flowers that grew in the flower bed next to her bedroom window. She left the window open at night, against her uncle's wishes, in order to receive the sweet aroma they gave each morning.

She touched the lilies and then the sunflowers as she let the petals run through her fingers. She then thought about the guy who she ran into the other day and the way he had embraced her touch when he shook her hand.

It had been a while since she had had a man in her life. Ever since Ricco was murdered, she found her days spent running the club and hanging out with her lesbian friends. So maybe this wasn't a coincidence, she thought while breaking a piece of the sunflower from its stem and bringing it to her lips. She pulled her drapes after closing her window and then reached for her purse next to her bed to retrieve the card that read "24-Hour Service as Needed."

She thought for a minute as she lay back on the bed looking up at the ceiling. Her T-shirt rose just below the base of her nipples, exposing her beautiful smooth stomach that showed a diamond stud that was pierced through her navel. She rubbed on it as if it was a crystal ball, giving her insight on what to do next. She suddenly realized that the answer was coming from the swell of her mound as she began to touch herself. Jai noticed the wet spot in the center of her boy shorts and threw the card on the floor as she stormed to the bathroom to jump into the shower.

It was late in the afternoon when she jumped in her car and found herself driving down Pico on her way to the club. She expected to see her uncle when she got there, but no one was there besides her and Jimmy.

Jimmy arrived early that day to take a liquor count for their opening that weekend. Young Geezee was showing up at the VIP lounge, so she knew that business was going to be popping.

Jimmy stood at the front door in his skinny jeans and T-shirt looking like a modern-day J.J. from *Good Times*. Jai loved talking with him. He kept her laughing with his arsenal of jokes. What was even funnier was the crush that he had on Octavia. She was a little too fast for him, plus she liked women. But it was always cute how he showed interest in her every time he saw her.

"What's up, Jai? Octavia coming this week? She got to see me DJ for Young Geezee," he said.

"Now you know Octavia don't like no Young Geezee!" she told him while unlocking the door. "So if she does come, she's coming to see you, crazy boy!"

Jai went through the front door while Jimmy followed behind her. She loved making him feel good.

Once they were inside, Jai headed to the back of the club while Jimmy slid behind the bar to restock the liquor.

The place was cold and still as Jai entered her office. But she knew that before the week's end the place was going to be cracking like Jay-Z's 40/40 Club.

It was dark inside when she walked into her office. The only lights came from the computer screen as it illuminated the desk where she spent most of her time. It was at her computer that she made sure that every time she opened up for business, it was going to be popping. Whether it was from the celebs or just the DJ, she wanted to make sure that she had the best of the best. And if her uncle had to pay for it, at least she knew that the club hoppers would leave there with a stain on their brains.

Jai sat down at her desk. She hit a few buttons on the keyboard, and the lights came on. She could see Jimmy dancing to his tunes while working and making sure that the shot glasses were in order. Jai watched him and smiled as he did his signature move. She knew that he would never get a chance with Octavia, but she felt good that he was there with her.

Looking at the futon against the wall reminded her of the episode a week ago with the man in the suit. She listened to her uncle and made sure that she was never alone in the club, and that all the security cameras were always on. Que never told her the real reason for the precaution, but she knew her uncle well enough to take his word at face value.

She jumped when the phone rang, answering it before it rang a second time. Her voice cracked as she said hello while still looking at the futon. It bothered her that a total stranger with a gun had gotten that close to her, and could have easily ended her life if he wanted to. But she was happy when she heard the familiar voice on the other end of the line, which brought a smile to her face.

"Hey, Uncle Que! I finally get a chance to talk to you. Are you okay?"

"Are you at the club?"

"Yes, I'm here. Jimmy is here with me setting up. Are you coming by?"

She knew very well that he was not, but she figured she would ask anyway.

"Nah, baby girl! Once again, everything is in ya hands. Your uncle got some business to handle." He paused. "You be careful."

"You always got some business to take care of," she repeated, looking away from the futon and back again at the computer. "What's going on? The last couple of times I talked to you, you've sounded shaky. And you never told me about the man in the suit who came by asking about you, might I add, with a gun in his waist," she said as her fingers pounded on the keyboard. "Are you in some kind of trouble or something?" she continued until he responded.

"Listen, when the time is right, I'll stop by and run it all down to you. But right now, I just need you to be careful and keep ya antennae up like I always taught you," he said as he looked at the front door of the club through his binoculars from across the street.

He spotted the Benz that he had bought her and smiled.

"You know that I would never put you in harm's way. Even when you think I'm not there, I got ya back!"

"But I want to have your back, too, Unc! What's up?"

"And you do! By helping me run the club," he told her as he looked at his Rolex. "Just remember what I said and be safe."

"I will. You too!" she begged before hanging up.

She then looked at the bar and made herself a drink. But just as she began to put the ice in her glass, she decided against it.

"It's too early for this! Drinking this early is for losers or for those that got their money right, and right now I'm neither."

She stepped out of her office and passed the lounge area.

"Hey, Jimmy, gotta make a run. Can you hold it down while I'm gone?" she yelled, and was out of the door before he could respond.

It was just another day at the gym for Heath as he lifted the four wheels of Olympic iron from the floor. It was like old times when the three of them used to work out together on the third floor of Iron'RE's mansion in Canada. The snow would fall as they watched from the inside while buffing iron. But now it was just the two of them, because one decided to go against the grain.

"Push it!" Iron'RE said as Heath was finishing his last set. He grabbed a towel to wipe the sweat from his forehead. "You know that Que is the reason I'm with you today," he said, dropping the towel to the floor.

"I remember when I first came to Canada to meet you," Heath said as he recalled the first encounter with Que that ultimately changed his life.

* * *

He never had seen Vancouver before except on the big screen, until one day after a few get-togethers. Que asked him to make a run with him as they drove through Seattle by truck to cross the Canadian border. It was easy for Que because he had taken this ride many times before. But Heath endured the long ride with questions. Que filled him in only on what he needed to know, and he assured him that his safety was secure.

When they made it through the border, he was fascinated with the majestic mountains. They were dipped in the icy snow as the crystal-blue waters danced around them, glistening while the evergreen, spruce, and sycamore trees swayed side to side from the easy breeze.

"Hey, Que, I always caught this spot on TV. I've seen it on *National Geographic*, but never like this! In 3D, my nigg! You doin' the most!"

"Yeah, it's a beauty, ain't it?"

Heath stuck his head out the window to get a better view of the scenery that seemed a little too real. He choked on the crisp air that pressed against his face as the truck continued its speed.

"Shit! It's cold as hell out there, my boy!"

"I should have told you this shit ain't no Cali weather. It's like twenty degrees out there right now," Que announced. "That's why I got us these special coats. Take a look in the back."

Heath jumped in the back and found a plastic casing hanging just above the refrigerator. He saw two black leather coats inside just like Que had said. Together they weighed at least ten pounds, and they were laced in polar bear wool.

"What's this?" he said to himself. "Sable? Burberry?"

As he looked inside, he saw that it was London Fog, a very expensive piece of leather. When he jumped back to the front, Heath had a disappointed looked on his face.

Earlier in the day, Que had told him about the freight they were carrying. It was $2 million in small bills wrapped in plastic and concealed in two English rugs. But as he was going through the coats, he came across an envelope with his name on it. Inside were three photos. One was of a man who he did not recognize, while the second photo was of a house with the address on the back. The last picture was of the same man with a circle around his head. On the back it read: "Terminate . . . $30,000."

Que turned to look at Heath and saw the perplexed look on his face.

"You found them? Good!"

He put his hazards lights on as he pulled over to the right

shoulder, before coming to a complete stop.

"Wait a minute!" Que said before jumping out to set the orange cones behind the truck according to regulations.

Que had a way with words, and he knew the right things to say in order to get anybody to do just as he wished. Besides, he had the money to influence others. So it wasn't hard to convince Heath to collect $30,000 in cash for putting the hammer to somebody.

"Look here," he said while getting back into the truck. "You know what it is, baby boy. Since you met me, you have seen the real me, and you know I'm no joke. I mean, come on, bro. Look where I got you!" he continued, sweeping his arms around and observing the scenery. "We in Canada, my boy!"

Heath looked at him, amazed at how beautiful this place was.

"Yeah, I know, bro, but put me up on game. Don't just leave me in the blinds like this," he added while looking at the envelope in his hand. "What's these pics for?"

"Look, baby boy. I'm taking you to meet the man. He's from India, and they call him Iron'RE. The boy's off money, business, and steroids."

Heath looked around.

"I told him about you and how you have no problem getting blood on ya face. And $30,000, boy! One hit and you ain't gotta rob no banks no more. Them things are janky anyway!"

Heath was surprised when he heard the proposition, but even more surprised that he had to doubt Que, since his rep ran a long ways in the streets. After hearing everything that Que had told him, he understood why he was in so deep. His whole operation was like an old mafia script.

They pulled up to what looked like a three-story mansion that was secluded in the woods. The scenery was majestic and surrounded the glass mansion with snowy hills. Impressions from wildlife hooves were all over the ground that shared the residence.

The ground was covered in snow as they drove up the horseshoe-like driveway. Big men in suits were waiting for them out front of the house, since they knew ahead of time of their arrival.

"Don't fret, baby boy. Just a few of the kids to give us a warm welcome," he told him. "We fam out here. Sometimes I stay out here for a while to look after his wife, Lisa, when he's away on business."

Heath just sat there taking it all in. The inside of his palms began to itch, and he just knew he was about to be on.

"What do I gotta do?" he asked.

"All ya gots to do is knock someone down. I got the location you need right there," he said as he pointed to the envelope that was still in Heath's hand. "A favor for Iron'RE and $30,000 in cash when you're done."

"How did you get the info?"

"Good question, but don't trip on that. Iron'RE can find anybody no sweat!"

"Where the hit gonna be?"

"Back in the Colonies. Now, let's go meet the man!"

* * *

Iron'RE grabbed the one-hundred-pound dumbbells and set them on his knees.

"Yeah, I remember when you came up. You did that little thing for me, and it made front-page news: 'Car forced off road by gunfire. Driver uninjured,' the papers read. You missed your mark, but Canada never saw shit like that before," he said.

They both laughed as Iron'RE went down on his set.

"You redeemed yourself though when you went back to Cali, and I liked that."

75

"And I liked how you looked out for me ever since, Iron'RE. When I did those ten years, sometimes I didn't know how I was gonna make it. But the cards your wife sent me, and all the love with them, kept a brother with hope."

"Glad to hear that."

"I knew once I got out that I didn't wanna live that life no more. I spent so many days in solitude thinking about getting me a good woman and kicking back with some lil' ones—a bunch of them lil' bastards," he said as Iron'RE almost dropped the weights to the floor, cracking up while he listened to his boy profess his dreams.

Iron'RE recalled reading the letters he wrote over the years and witnessing his growth. He was a man of great learning himself, and always approved of anyone learning on a higher level to improve their livelihood.

"My bad, bro. Didn't mean to laugh. It's just that I remember you used to be a major player, and now you talking about kids. That's what's up!" he said as he wiped the sweat from his forehead and took off his wifebeater and wiped off his chest.

A young lady walked by smiling while she admired his tattooless body, captivated by his bulk and chiseledness. Iron'RE then looked back at Heath.

"But now, up close, just being with you these past few days, I can see the change," he said while reaching down to grab his water bottle. "You know I'm not trying to drag you back into this life. I only told you about Que because I know that's your boy, and I know that you will help me find him because of your loyalty."

"Ya know I got ya back. You've been there for me through hard times and some more!" Heath admitted.

* * *

As they left the gym and stepped out into the parking lot, they both headed for their cars. The lot was beginning to fill up at the twenty-four-hour fitness club as other cars pulled into the stalls. Heath made a hand gesture as Iron'RE smiled and then laughed.

Just as Iron'RE got to his car, he saw a suspicious van in the corner that he swore he had seen before. The blue paint was fading from the sides as if it had been sitting in the sun for years. The front two windows were tinted, as well as the windshield, but he could still see someone moving inside as he got closer. His eyes zeroed in on the shadowy figure as he approached. He could almost see the smirk on his face.

Iron'RE got closer before the engine came alive and then shots rang out.

Pop! Pop! Pop!

A bullet passed his ear as he ducked behind two parked cars.

Pop! Pop! Pop!

The shattered glass from the window refused to let Iron'RE get up to return fire. He stayed low with gun in hand, ready to return fire, but it was too late. The faded van took off, with the wheels screeching the pavement.

Iron'RE stood there as the back of the van disappeared into traffic. Before he knew it, Heath was at his side with gun in hand, concealing it under his shirt. He jumped when Heath touched his shoulder, not from being scared but more from being snapped out of the vision of what he wanted to do to Que once he caught up with him.

"I'm pretty sure that was Que."

"Ya think?" Heath replied.

"I've seen that van before, Heath. I believe I purchased that van a year ago to dispose of something but ended up never using it."

"Are you straight, Iron'RE? Did you get hit anywhere?" Heath asked, looking over his boy to make sure that there were no bullet holes.

He looked at Heath and took his eyes off the direction that the van went.

"No, I'm fine! I want you to continue to keep tabs on his niece," Iron'RE began. "And be careful. If that was him, then he may have seen you as well."

Iron'RE headed back to his car while onlookers began to pass by, curious about what had just happened.

"I'll call you later. I got a plan," he announced before driving off.

* * *

Once he got onto Ocean Boulevard, Que drove west until he got onto Interstate 710 and entered the on-ramp. He thought about taking Iron'RE out when he had the chance, but it just seemed too easy. In fact, it seemed way too easy for the don to be slipping like that, he thought.

He knew that he should have started gunning at his target. In fact, he almost did until he spotted Heath, his old-school partner. So he let off some distracting rounds to make it look like he was trying to do some damage, in order to give him some time to get out of there. When he saw Heath coming to his rescue, he knew that he was sure to give chase.

"I put you in the game!" he said to himself as his knuckles turned white from the tight grip of the wheel. "When the hell did you get out?"

They both did dirty together when Heath joined the team. The body count between the two of them was more than Sammy the Bull's. And with time and multiple hits, Heath had become a trained killer. Que knew that if he had killed Iron'RE right there, Heath wouldn't have let him get out of that parking lot alive.

Iron'RE drove in silence as he cruised the highway thinking about the episode that had just taken place. He realized that his life easily had been on the verge of being taken had his instincts not kicked in. He recognized the van from the jump, and he knew that Que was inside. Either that or he had hired someone to do his dirty work. He wasn't scared at all.

He approached the van knowing that one of two things was going to happen. He would die today or the person behind that wheel would live to see another day, but those days would be numbered. Although it wasn't a joke, he smiled as he replayed the scene, admiring his keen senses, even though now he was in his mid-forties.

He had been in the game a long time, and he knew that he didn't have to be any longer. He could have just as well left everything alone and taken off with his wife to live on an island in the middle of nowhere. That's how long his paper was.

But there was something about loyalty that just didn't sit well with him when it was betrayed. And that's what kept him ticking.

That's what kept the body counts rising in his world. Because when you betrayed Iron'RE, there were no limits he wouldn't go to just to find you and let you know, in the worst way, that you had made a big mistake. His smile slowly faded as he approached the restaurant at which he was going to stop.

Aware of the LA traffic, Iron'RE carefully turned into M&M's Soul Food place, on the corner of Crenshaw and Martin Luther Boulevards. There was a theme with all three names that were known to represent the accomplishments of Black America.

This particular corner was just one of the local monuments that showed unity in a race that had suffered many atrocities in the course of developing such a culture. The area was known for maintaining the integrity of the generations before them, with showcases of black-owned businesses surrounded by 1950s-style homes that were well taken care of with their manicured lawns.

Iron'RE enjoyed this place each time he came to the city. He loved the aura of this Black community. The hospitality that it gave, even to a foreigner like him, made him feel at home each time he came to visit. Although it would be a while between each of his visits, Iron'RE never seemed to forget the names of those that left good impressions.

The lot was a tight one when he pulled in, squeezing his 550 Benz between two parked cars. Luckily the car on this driver's side was just leaving, with a heavy-set woman who looked like she had just gotten out of church. She waved with a smile as she backed out of the parking lot. This was in the good part of LA, he thought to himself, where total strangers did gestures of kindness.

Iron'RE jumped out of his car in just his sweats and wifebeater. The long Mongolian braid fell down the middle of his back between his broad shoulders, which stood out just like his biceps. With his West Indies looks and the physique of a bodybuilder, Iron'RE always had a reason for the women to engage in conversation, usually inquiring about his geographic background. Although he obliged on many occasions, Iron'RE remained strong in his commitment to his wife, Lisa. Because there was something about loyalty, and his family shunned betrayal; he therefore stayed loyal.

But when it came to Lula, he opened the doors to certain flirtations, knowing that no boundaries would be crossed.

It had been a few years since he had been there. And as he walked inside, she greeted him as such with a kiss on the cheek and a strong embrace as she came from behind the counter.

"Iron'RE, what a surprise!"

Her perfume lingered. Coco Chanel, he thought as she released him and cupped his hand in hers while she led them to their favorite table—the place they would sit and converse every time.

As they moved through the restaurant, he waved at the other girls behind the counter, who giggled, well aware of the crush that Lula had on Iron'RE. As they sat down, one of the girls came over to take his order, which was the same every time: collard greens, cornbread, and a side order of chitterlings.

The girl took his order and left as they began to chat. Lula giggled and blushed as Iron'RE sat with his elbows crossed on the table as his lips moved. He admired her chocolate skin, big-bubbled eyes, and the dimples in her cheeks when her face smiled. She was beautiful inside and out.

He often referred to her as being his second wife. In fact, his wife, Lisa, knew all about their friendship, as the two Skyped almost every day.

Lula had come from a rough childhood, and escaped the world of gang life and prostitution, although her mother had gotten turned out. On Iron'RE's first visit, he had fallen in love with her personality. And after hearing her story, he offered to pay for her to be a full-time student at USC to become a lawyer, which was her dream. Lula vowed to help those that became victims of physical abuse and human trafficking. This was the main quality that attracted Iron'RE to her. The gift she possessed of helping others.

As he paid for his food, he gave Lula another kiss on the cheek, wishing her well. He didn't know when he would see her physically again, but he knew that she was able to contact him any time if necessary.

When he climbed into his car, his mind shifted just as quickly. He thought about a plan to get to Que, and he knew that he had to move fast.

He made a left out into traffic and then another left at the light, before making a quick right back onto Martin Luther Boulevard. He then went beneath the underpass near the Crenshaw Mall.

He drove until he made his way to Baldwin Hills, where he was the owner of a home that he occupied when he came to the States. The area was a community of old-fashioned homes that were owned by famous people from the '60s and '70s. They were now left behind for the working class who could afford them.

He pulled up into a winding driveway overshadowed by trees, and got out of the car with food in hand. The house was a huge one story with five bedrooms and a spacious living room, with some of the finest furniture you could buy. Although he was hardly there, the inside still resembled the coziness of a full-time family home.

As he set down the food on the kitchen counter, he went into the bedroom to change and take a shower. He thought about Que again and the total disregard of his actions in the parking lot at the gym. He was surprised that Que had acted as wildly as he did, instead of maintaining the discipline that he was taught when it came time to kill.

"Hell!" he said under his breath. "You may have been successful had you just gotten off with a silencer and the element of surprise."

He laughed as he silenced the water with the turn of the knob, and walked around dripping wet throughout the house as he dried off. He opened up the plate of food while sliding on a pair of boxers, before taking it into the den to relax.

His favorite move was *Menace to Society*. He loved the part when Kane stumped out old boy in front of his house over some dispute with the guy's sister. At the end of the movie, the guy got revenge with the element of surprise by catching Kane slipping and then killing him off.

Something similar could have happened to him that day, he thought as he sat down to watch the movie. But he made an oath to himself to never get caught slipping like that again. As he looked at his phone, a thought came to mind, and he made a call to JoJo.

JoJo was in his apartment complex pumping iron while Tupac's *Me Against the World* album banged from his radio. He ran the Jungles, a community of apartment complexes that sat in the center of Baldwin Hills.

There was only one way in and one way out of this place, with streets that ran bowlegged. This meant that if you did not know where you were going, you could end up at a dead end. And being in that situation at a particular time of the night could cause you to become victimized by dangerous gang members that were notorious in that neighborhood.

JoJo was one of the South Central kids that ran Iron'RE's operations in this district. He was short but stocky and built like a linebacker with cock-strong strength. One of the qualities that

Iron'RE liked when they first met was JoJo's skills of boxing and martial arts. It came with humbleness and discipline that he knew often got tested with crushing results—and sometimes deadly ones. He was a chameleon, but you couldn't recognize the change until it happened. This was Iron'RE's secret weapon.

He was on his third set when his phone rang.

"Yo, what's up, pops?"

He always spoke this way when he got a call from this number.

"Fo' sho', you want me to put some work in on the transition?"

JoJo knew exactly what was up as Iron'RE spoke through the phone. He knew who Que was, and knew that he wasn't hard to find. He would just hit the streets to get a few questions answered and complete the mission, and hopefully make his pops proud. When he hung up the phone, he went inside to make a call.

JoJo called Spider, a local gang member with the Bloods organization that was heavy into the streets. He knew all the club scenes and functions that took place within the proximity of their domain, which included all the streets throughout LA. Spider wasn't one of the kids, but he was one of JoJo's road dawgz from childhood. He shared the same ambition as JoJo, and that was to be rich and successful by all means possible.

In order to find Spider, you would have to look in some of the most unusual places. When it came to business working from Monday through Friday, Spider could be found in his office in the Wilshire District, running his contractor business from a one hundred-floor high-rise, overlooking the streets of Beverly Hills. But his working attire was in total contrast to the red Chuck Taylors and black khakis that he sported on the weekends.

He and JoJo shared the same traits when it came to being a chameleon as he sat behind his desk in his comfortable leather chair in slacks, a dress shirt, and suspenders. From the looks of the office, and the man that sat behind the desk, no one would believe that he was a real-live gang member that took pride in what he did, whether it was selling dope, putting in work, or supporting parolees with a job in construction, all for the benefit of the community.

JoJo wasn't surprised as he stepped through the door to greet his road dawg, because as a teen, he planted the seed. And as he became acquainted with Iron'RE, and getting on his payroll, he began to water this dream that included Spider.

"What up, baby boy?"

He closed the door and met Spider in the middle of his office with an embrace.

"How's biz going in this bitch?" he asked with a smile, proud of how far they had come.

Spider walked over to his desk and offered JoJo a seat as he got comfortable. Neither one drank alcohol, because they both believed that it obscured their judgment. And in their line of work, they had to stay sharp. So Spider handed his boy the water bottle that he had waiting for him on his desk.

"Business is cracking, man! I just low-key landed a contract for that new stadium at the Hollywood Park. That's another one hundred jobs for the Black man just gettin' outta prison looking for that work," he explained, taking a big sip of water. "What you got going on?" he asked, after twisting the cap back on before putting it on the desk.

JoJo stood up from the chair and admired the photos on the wall that he had seen a hundred times before.

"I got a call from Iron'RE."

"Oh yeah?"

"Yeah, he's down here in LA and says he got some work for us.

Some trash that needs to be taken out!"

He walked over to one of the photos on the wall. It was a picture of the two of them at Spider's graduation from Southwest Community College, where he started on his degree in business.

"I need ya help on this one, my boy," he said with a smile while looking back at him.

"Say no more, my boy! What ya got?"

JoJo was never surprised at his readiness, and he knew that this drive, ambition, and being down for whatever was what got them to where they were today. So why stop? He then smiled at Spider.

"Ya know, you a crazy SOB, my boy!"

As he walked back over to the chair to sit down, he said, "Do you remember our boy Que?"

"Yeah! He was one of the sharpest and most accurate thugs in Iron'RE's operation."

But he was surprised to hear his name as being part of the trash or anything for that matter. JoJo caught his expression.

"Yeah, I know. Iron'RE wants to air him out. He said he capped at him the other day!" he explained after taking another swig from the water bottle and sitting down. "I don't know how that happened.

All I know is that he wants us to smash, so that's what we gonna do, ya dig?"

"I can dig it, but ya know that dude ain't easy to get at."

"I know, but don't you still fuck with one of his pieces? What's that crazy bitch's name? The bi chick?"

"Oh, you talking about that chick Kayla? Fo' sho! She be at the Catch. I see ol' girl all the time, bro!"

"Well, get at her and see what's up with Que. We gotta find dude quick and close the book, ya dig?"

JoJo got up from his chair.

"I'll see my way out and let you get back to business," he said as he threw the water bottle into the trash on the way to the door. "Holla at ya later, bro!" he said as he walked out the door and shut it behind him.

Spider sat down at his desk thinking about the task at hand. He had Kayla's phone number in his contacts on one of his phones that he kept at his office for reasons only he knew. And anytime Kayla got a call from this number, she would answer with no hesitation.

* * *

Kayla was infatuated with Spider. From his tattoos to his bullet wounds, this was one image that she dreamt about.

To be in the presence of Spider's massive build and six-foot frame came with an impression that she found fascinating. He only had one eye. Most people would have seen this as a handicap, but Spider wore it as a badge of honor. And as they lay together after rough sex one night, she asked the million-dollar question.

"What happened to your eye?"

He told her about the steel-toed boot that caught him in the face during a brawl of six on one that left him unconscious. When he added that he had come back and laid everything down, she was in puppy love.

Reaching into an unlocked cabinet, he grabbed the phone that he was looking for. It was an old Motorola phone that he used to store contacts that were for certain usage.

As he opened up the screen, he scrolled down until he found her name.

"Hey, baby girl!" he said while smiling as he looked down at the street below.

Heath lay on his couch watching recorded episodes of the hit series "Southland." His condo was immaculate for a bachelor. The living room was decorated with exquisite wood and soft leather, with a 90-inch flat-screen cornered by black sectional couches draped with cream-colored throw pillows.

On the wall above it he had a wide portrait of a bare-chested man being fed grapes by three beautiful women. Heath considered this to be an icebreaker most of the time when he entertained company. The women would say that it should be the other way around, with him feeding them grapes. But when the sun came up, they would have a change of heart.

There was another painting displayed among the others on the wall next to the kitchen that stood out on its own. It was a portrait of Tupac Shakur on a suede canvas, framed in caramel-shellacked oak wood. He had picked up the picture in Tijuana for only $5, but he knew that some day it would be worth hundreds of thousands.

On his back was a tattoo of a prison tower surrounded by barbed wire and walls riddled with bullet holes. It was silhouetted with a face that resembled his. The words on the wall stated, "My life no more, but no regrets."

He had the ink done in prison and put it on his back to put the past behind him. But he wanted the whole world to see where he had come from and where he was going. But with the mess that Que had him in now, he knew that the reason for that tattoo would have to be put on hold.

His phone rang. As he answered it, he saw the name on the caller ID and smiled.

On the other end was Summer, who sounded as sexy as ever, using his name with an exaggerated tone.

"What's up, Heeeeath? Can I come over? I'm horny as fuck!"

Heath had to laugh at that, because he knew that Summer was a hot mess. Ever since he had put it on her, she couldn't get enough of him. She was a sexy little thing who only went out with cats for their money, and Heath knew it.

So one day he took her to the Beverly Center to shop at Victoria's Secret and bought her all types of lingerie and expensive bras. He kept the tags on the expensive merchandise and put them in the trunk of his car before they drove to the Freeway Inn Hotel. Once they got there, he took her inside had smashed. Afterward, she asked to try on the lingerie. Heath went back to the car to get it, only never to return. Heath took the pieces back to the store for a refund and hadn't seen her since. He was surprised to get a call from her a week later, forgiving him for being so scandalous. It had actually turned her on.

She told him that no one had ever done her like that before; and although she was mad, she had to smile at the fact that somebody had outsmarted her. She wondered why she was so infatuated with this man after what he had done, and suddenly realized that part of the reason was his body. The man had muscles like an Arabian horse. And the way he seduced her that night only magnified her desires. He knew all the right places to kiss and all the right places to touch. She just knew that she couldn't let this young stud go.

"What's up with ya crazy ass, Summer?" Heath asked as he got up from his couch and headed to his kitchen to get a bottle of water. "What you been up to?"

"Can I come over?" Summer begged in a way that made it seem as if she was already touching herself.

A few months ago, Heath would have obliged her with satisfaction. But the truth of the matter was that he was beginning to have feelings for Jai, and he realized this after meeting her in front of the club. He really wanted to get to know her better. So when it came to Summer, he had to decline for now.

"Summer, I'm going to take a rain check on this one," he said as he waited for her reply, only to initially hear deep sighs of disappointment. "Hit ya up later though," he concluded with a smile on his face, knowing that he wouldn't.

"All right, Heath, you sexy bastard. I'll be waiting for your call."

"For sure, baby girl! Take care of yourself," he ended, before hanging up the phone.

He went back to the couch to continue his relaxation as he looked at the picture on the wall—the one with the three goddesses—when he had a premonition.

"Dawg! What ya tripping off of!" he said out loud. "Summer's a straight fuck!"

He was about to call her back, until his phone started ringing, snapping him back to reality. It rang with no special ringtone, just the ordinary ring that every Sprint phone came with. He answered on the third ring to nothing but silence. He said hello again, but there was still silence on the other end.

He was about to hang up when it suddenly dawned on him.

"Jai, is that you?"

The phone still remained silent.

"Is everything okay?" he asked, waiting for a response, hoping it was her.

After a few moments of the existing silence, a voice finally broke through.

"Hello! Is this Heath?" a shy voice asked.

Yet as he heard it, he could feel the butterflies take over his body. He had this strange anxiety of wanting her right that very moment. He felt somewhat guilty at first, but relieved to know that wanting her had no shame. He decided that it wasn't selfish to take something that was rightfully his to have—and that was love.

"Are you okay?" he asked again.

"Yeah, I'm fine. Why?"

Heath didn't know how to respond. He wanted to go with his gut and dive right in, but he needed to be careful. It was a plus that she called, he thought, but he still didn't know the reason why. For all he knew, Que could have been on the other end listening in, trying to get the ups on him for the kill.

Heath knew all too well about that because he had done it many times before himself. And if that was the reason that she was calling, then he was game. He would just have to chalk this love shit up as a loss and make them both suffer. But if she was really worth it, then he would step out there only because his heart told him to, knowing that this could be the perfect opportunity to get close to her.

"Listen, can you get away for a few hours? I was just about to go get something to eat. Now that I have your attention, I was wondering if you'd let me feed you," he started as he got up to put on a shirt as he continued talking. "I was thinking about McDonald's. You with it?" he asked with a smile.

She giggled inside at the sound of Mickey D's. It was almost child-like to ask a girl out to a restaurant where they sold Happy Meals. Yet she was amused by the fact that he thought to include her along with his appetite.

"Does it have to be McDonald's?" she asked. "I mean, I can take a kid there."

"Okay, then you pick a spot. Your choice. Just make sure the food is good!"

* * *

It was already late in the afternoon when he saw her. He spotted her from the stoplight sitting in her car in the parking lot of the Sizzler restaurant on Manchester and Perri Avenue.

He smiled when he saw it, since the place brought back memories. The last time that he remembered being there was when the Lakers played at the Forum, which was across the street from where Jai was sitting. His mom, bless her heart, brought the family there for dinner after the game. It was the one opportunity that Heath had to get up close to Kareem Abdul-Jabbar.

She looked good to him—real good. Her hair was long, straight, and silky as it bounced off the sun's reflection. She wore no makeup, which insinuated her natural beauty.

Her embrace was a warm one, but it was unexpected when Heath jumped out of this car. It caught him off guard at first. But when he gave in, he couldn't help but notice how long she stayed there.

"Are you okay?" he asked, pulling her away softly to look her in the face.

"I'm fine," she answered, finally breaking her embrace as she tugged at his hand to go inside. "That cologne smells good. What is it?" she asked, holding his hand tighter before giving it a second thought.

"Never mind. Come on, lunch is on me."

She took a seat near the window to look outside. They both watched as the groundskeepers tended to the landscaping around the cemetery across the street. Beautiful flowers were left behind on tombstones for loved ones that were no longer here.

He watched as she looked out the window while her hands fiddled with the ketchup dispenser.

"You have family there?" he asked.

The question surprised her and brought her out of her reverie.

"I'm sorry, was it that obvious?"

"You know, I went there once as a kid," he began. "They used to have this contest on Halloween. Whoever could get through the cemetery without falling through a hole won $100!"

They both said the last two words in unison.

"Yeah, I can remember correctly. Those that fell in the holes were assed out," Heath said.

He then recalled the story of how he went one Halloween night with a group of friends and only two of them made it out. He was one of the less fortunate ones that literally had to spend the night with Stacey, a girl who he landed on who was dressed like Aurora, the Roman goddess of dawn.

They both laughed at the story as Heath continued to charm her with the details of that night.

He was dressed as Goldie, a real-life pimp from the twentieth century. He was decked out in a neon yellow shirt that was tucked into a pair of Now and Later apple green bell-bottoms, and looking real debonair.

"I thought I was the shit that night. We pulled up in my grandma's '79 Coupe. I jumped out in my pimp shoes like an old boy in the movie *I'm Gonna Git You, Sucka!* Remember that?"

Jai broke out laughing, trying to picture him in the '80s looking like a pimp in neon clothing. She was impressed with the story, but she was more relieved to know that wasn't the image he was trying to portray right now.

He was glad that he was able to amuse her with his story. He found it to be a good icebreaker. And filling her belly would be a plus; he hoped that it would leave a stain on her brain.

They sat and talked through the platter of all-you-can-eat shrimp and a steak with salad. Neither realized how fast the time had gone by as they both enjoyed the food and conversation.

"You know, my twin brother is over there," she said.

"Oh! I didn't know!"

"He died from an asthma attack when we were young."

"When was the last time you visited?"

"I go every year. Today is the anniversary of his death," she told him. "I was planning on going over there after we finished here to lay flowers."

Heath studied her for a minute and realized why she had picked this restaurant. It was close to the place where her brother rested.

It was also the first time he heard of the brother, and wondered if Que was coming to join her. If so, then he knew that his cover could be blown.

"I don't have anything to do after this. Are you going alone? Any other family coming?"

"No, I always go alone. My mom lives in Oakland. She couldn't stand to look at the streets of LA after he died. My uncle is the one who buried him here," she said.

"It must have been hard on her," Heath said as Jai looked out the window once more. "What about ya uncle, what's his name?"

"Who, Que?"

"Right, Que. Does he come to visit your brother?"

"My uncle is a busy man. He stays on the go. Que believes that money can fix everything. Like I said, he paid for the plot, and that was it."

She then turned to look at him and said, "But I love him for that. You can always count on him when you want something done."

Jai looked back at Heath, almost as if accusing him of something as Heath put his hand over hers.

"I don't have anything to do after this," he admitted once again. "I wouldn't mind accompanying you. That is, if you don't mind."

"You don't have to. I don't feel right in asking you to come to a cemetery."

"You didn't! I volunteered!"

She opened her mouth to protest, but he silently put a finger to her lips to quiet her.

"Look, I understand what you're going through right now, and unless you want to be alone, I wouldn't mind coming," he said while looking into her eyes and witnessing the confusion that still lingered. "Are you enjoying my company right now?"

She nodded with an inquiring look that confirmed everything that he was thinking inside.

"I got no other place that I'd rather be than right here in this moment."

Her blush was open, for everyone to see.

Heath leaned in close, caressing both hands as he spoke. As he did, he couldn't help but notice the cute little boy who stood up in his booth just behind them, with a beautiful innocent smile. He had premature curly hair, with bubbly brown eyes to die for. With his look of approval, the little boy sacralized the union between the two.

"Looks like you have an admirer," Heath said.

Jai turned around to look. She couldn't help but pinch the chubby cheeks of the young kid as they blew up when he smiled.

"I'm so sorry," the young boy's mother replied.

"No worries!" Heath said. "I been doing the same thing since I met her and haven't been able to stop!" he said as he looked back at Jai and then at the boy. "What's his name?"

"This is my son, Lil' Sampson. He's two years old," the mother said while holding him in her arms. "Oh, by the way, you two are a beautiful couple."

"Well, thank you. And when he gets old enough, tell Lil' Sampson that he has beautiful taste in women," Heath responded as the mother smiled while collecting her things to leave.

"You are so crazy!" Jai said, slapping his hand as he watched the boy and his mother get closer to the door. "Why you let ol' girl think that we were a couple like that?"

"What!" Heath turned to face her, smiling ear to ear. "What was I supposed to say. Ya know her son held us in secret matrimony!"

They both started to laugh as Heath held her hands.

He was still holding on to her hand as he walked her to the car. It was late in the evening now, and Jai couldn't remember the last time she enjoyed herself so much. She would go alone to the cemetery with a bottle of Cognac and drink with her twin, telling him all about the wonderful guy she had just met.

As they reached their cars, Heath opened the door for her while she climbed inside. He reached for her hand one last time, held it to his lips, and gave it a kiss.

"I enjoyed lunch with you today."

Jai blushed and let out a low, "Oh my!" while cupping her mouth with her other hand, trying to hold her feelings inside. "It was nice," was all she could say before driving out of the parking lot and into traffic.

As Heath turned to walk to his car, he didn't see the car coming toward him, almost clipping him with the fender as his hand hit the hood.

"Hey, slow that shit down!" he yelled, but it was too late. The driver had already driven off in hot pursuit of the 550. "Hey, you mutha!"

* * *

Jai pulled up to the gate and passed through, following the winding road which led to her twin brother's place of rest. She parked on the side and reached for the bottle of Cognac.

No glasses this time. This year she would drink straight from the bottle and pour some on the ground for Jarrod.

Jai walked over to the plaque as she got out of the car and spread her blanket to sit down next to her brother. Flowers from the year before were still there, along with the, "We miss you, Jarrod, and always love you," note written in big, bold letters filled with hearts and kisses.

It was evident that he was very much loved and missed.

His uncle had gone all out with the marble brick and picture of his little nephew that read In Loving Memory.

Tears ran down her cheeks as she reminisced. The blunt she smoked with him last year was still there, obscured with a plastic container so that it wouldn't be disturbed. She knew that if he had been alive all this time, that Jarrod would have most definitely been her chiefing partner.

She reached for her phone and played Diana Ross's "Missing You" over and over as she knocked back the top and poured some to the ground.

"I miss you, too, bro."

The sun was just setting when she got home. When she pulled up into the driveway, she sat for a moment, thinking about how well her day had gone.

Jai wanted Heath to come to the cemetery with her, but she decided to wait. Her lunch date was going well, and she figured why mess it up by bringing a total stranger with her to watch her weep?

She was light-weight buzzing from the pint she drank earlier, smiling while she thought about the way that Heath held her hand to his lips. His scent lingered on her clothes from the moment they embraced, which left her smelling the air as she sat. She was already missing him.

The next day Heath followed Jai onto the 405 Freeway heading north. It looked as if she was heading to the LAX Airport, but he wasn't sure. She was driving calmly this time, he thought, which was strange. Because all the other times he had been following her, she had been driving like Jimmy Johnson. He stayed three cars behind her to make sure that he went unseen. Although traffic was heavy, he wanted to take no chances on blowing his cover.

His phone began to ring just when he thought about calling her. He looked down at the screen to push the Accept button.

"What's up, Iron'RE?" he said with both hands on the wheel.

Iron'RE sat in front of his laptop on Skype while he viewed the other side of the screen.

"Oh, looks like you in heavy traffic, huh?"

"Yeah, got ya girl like three cars ahead of me. Looks like she's heading to LAX. Don't know fo' sho' though."

"LAX, huh? Wonder if she's going to meet Que?"

"Don't know. I was gonna call her just before you called, hoping that's what he was going to tell me. If so, I was going to throw his ass in the trunk."

"Sounds like a plan," Iron'RE said. "But stay on ya p's and q's. He may have seen you at the gym with me the other day."

Iron'RE looked around before speaking as if no was listening.

"Plus, I got my ears to the streets as we speak. I got JoJo looking into something for me. But like I said, be careful!"

"I got ya, RE. But like I said, she's leading me to him. He's in the trunk to be delivered to you like FedEx." He laughed. "Let me hit up ol' girl to find out what she really has going on, and then I'll hit ya back."

"Do that, my friend. Talk to ya later," Iron'RE said before hanging up.

"All right, let's see where you're headed, Flower," he said to himself as he started to dial her number.

But just as his fingers got to the contacts, his phone began to ring. He looked down at the screen and then hit the Accept button.

"How can I help you?"

Jai was blushing from the sound of his voice.

"Look at you! All business-like!" she said. "Do you have room on ya plate . . . I mean schedule . . . for a girl?"

She had to rephrase the last sentence. Although she wouldn't have minded being one of his favorite dishes, she didn't want to sound thirsty.

"How you doing? I thought that was you. What's good?" Heath inquired, not wanting to sound too thirsty himself.

He knew that it was Jai when the phone rang, since he had a special ringtone associated with her number once he added her to his contacts.

It wasn't easy following her and having feelings for her at the same time. When he got home from spending the day with her, he couldn't get the thought of her out of his brain. The way that cute little boy kept smiling at them, it was as if God was telling him that the two of them were meant for each other. What if she was the one, he thought, before speaking again?

"How you been, baby girl?"

"I guess you didn't hear my question," she said. "Never mind. I'm fine. How are you?"

Heath pulled over to the shoulder of the freeway and threw his hazard lights on. There was no need to follow her now that he had her on the phone.

"I was just at the office putting these oils together," he lied. "And, yes, I heard the question. The reason I didn't answer right away was because I wanted to let ya voice linger in the air awhile!"

He knew that they were both on even ground now.

"Oh wow!"

"Oh wow is right. That's how my day was with you the other day; and now here it is again that you bless me for the second time with that sweet melody."

"Are you for real, Heath?"

"Excuse me, come again?"

"You heard me. I said are you for real?" Her tone was soft but exaggerated.

He could hear the smile that cracked her lips.

"I heard you. I just like the way you say my name," he said. "And I am for real, Jai. How can I get on your fan base? Hell, with all that beauty surrounding you, I know you got more than a few."

She blushed inside as she listened to the words that were coming out of his mouth.

"That was cute. And thank you, but no!"

"But no, what?" he asked.

She smiled just as he did, but he made his known with laughter.

"No what, Jai?"

"No, I don't have any fans. Just a few friends that are women."

"Oh, what! You a southpaw? You go both ways?"

"Well as of today, I'm strictly dickly, but I have two bisexual friends who are my BFFs. I've known them for life."

He knew that she was speaking about Octavia and Kayla, and he wondered if she knew that he had taken the two of them down that night at the club. They were so gone that they might not have remembered their damn selves.

"So, what happened to the girl? The one you're not seeing no mo'?" he questioned.

She smiled as she thought about Blac Chyna.

"Well, let's just say it wasn't definite. I was just testing the waters, but that didn't happen. So I thought I'd just come home to my fine Black men."

"Good to hear that. To tell ya the truth, I didn't know just from looking at you," Heath said. "I don't know what's up with y'all women these days. It seems that all my sistas are chasin' the same anatomy. It's crazy!"

"All the good men are in prison. It's kinda hard finding that special one nowadays."

"Is that what happened to your dude? He went to prison?"

Jai got quiet for a minute. Everything was going good, she thought. But how did it come to this question? She wasn't expecting to get questioned about Ricco, her ex and first love who was gunned down. Sure, she was over him, but was it cool to divulge this information so soon to a guy she barely knew? But he was very handsome, in shape, and very manly in a gallant type of way. So who was she fooling, she wanted this man.

"No, the guy that I was stupid in love with was murdered over a year ago."

The way that she used the word sounded like it was punishment for the way Ricco treated her while they were together. It seemed that he twisted her up, not only physically but emotionally, and so much so that it was very hard to let him go even after he passed.

"Sorry to hear that," he told her.

"Look, can we talk about something else?" she asked, suddenly withdrawn.

But it was the words that came out of his mouth next that brought her back alive.

"Oh, how was the visit with your brother?"

"Oh, you remembered. Thank you, Heath. You're so sweet." Her smiled cracked again. "It was good. It's always a little sad, but good to be near him and think about the fun times we had."

Her exit was coming up, and she knew that she had to get off the phone so she could call her homegirl to let her know that she was close by.

"Look, I'm about to get off this freeway, so let me get off the phone. Can I call you back once I get to my friend's house?"

"Fo' sho', baby girl! Do that. Talk to ya later."

"Bye," she said, before hanging up to exit the freeway.

She took the Manchester exit and made a left turn, heading to a gated community where Octavia awaited her arrival.

Que lay back on his bed looking up at the ceiling. He contemplated the vision that he witnessed a few days ago in the Sizzler parking lot. He knew that his eyes weren't deceiving him. His old friend was indeed out of prison after ten years. He had heard that he was retiring from the game once he got out. He changed his life around, was going to church on the yard, and all that. So what was he doing with Iron'RE?

Que knew that Iron'RE was the type that lived by principles. And he knew, like Que, that if Heath wasn't in the life no more, then Iron'RE wouldn't pressure him to pick up a gun to go looking for him. But seeing him with Jai made his antennae go up. He had to make sure that Heath wasn't looking for him. But if he was, then he knew that he would have to kill him.

Kayla whispered in his ear: "What's on ya mind, boo?"

Her tongue nibbled on his earlobe, waking up the long snake between his legs. He hadn't worked out in months, but it was obvious from his physique that he was still in tip-top shape.

He grabbed her by the waist and lifted her on top of his phallus as it slid right into her wetness while he began to gyrate his hips, giving her every inch of him. She moaned in ecstasy each time her pelvis touched the bottom of his manhood.

"I love you, Que. Ohhh! I love you, boy!"

"That's right, boo. That's right!" he said as he pushed harder and harder, taking his frustration out on her piñata.

She screamed at the top of her lungs, the loudest they had ever been since they first started making love. She screamed so loud that she didn't hear her phone go off—not once, not twice, but three times—when the caller left a message.

After they were done, Que got up to use the bathroom while Kayla lay there looking up at the ceiling in a daze. Que put it on her this time, and it felt good. She had kept it a secret from her best friend for a long time now. Not even Octavia knew about their affair. And Que thought it should stay that way. But the words that she was screaming out while he was laying pipe had her feeling torn. She would keep it a secret, to herself for now, but she didn't know for how long.

While she continued to stare up at the ceiling, the sound of a beep brought her out of her reverie. She looked down at the floor at the side of the bed where her purse sat, and she reached for her phone. As she opened the screen, she realized that she had a message. She opened the phone up and put it to her ear to listen.

It had been almost two months since she had heard from Spider, and she was surprised when she heard his voice asking to return his call as soon as possible. He even used the word "urgent."

As the bathroom door swung open, she swiftly put the phone back into her purse, lifted back up with a blunt in her mouth, and lit it with a lighter in her hand all in one motion.

Kayla was good, but sometimes too good for her damn self. She thought she was smooth by putting her phone back into her purse and then producing a lighter to light her blunt as if that was what she was looking for.

At first, she couldn't understand why she was feeling guilty, that is, until she heard Spider's voice and realized that she had feelings for him, too.

On the other hand, Que wasn't working with feelings at all. It was just that her movements made her suspect. The last time she was at his place, she clipped his wallet for a few racks, thinking that he wouldn't miss it. Just as before, after making love, he left the room and came back, only to find that some of his cash was missing.

He walked over to the side of the bed where she lay.

"What ya doing?" he asked in a playful voice while reaching down for her purse.

She swatted his hand away, but he grabbed it, making her purse fall to the floor and causing her phone to spill out just as it was ringing. He picked it up to hand it to her, but paused when he saw the face on the screen. It was Spider calling back because she hadn't returned his call.

Que sat on the sofa at the foot of the bed with the phone in his hand as it continued to ring.

"Give me my phone, boy. What you doing?"

He started to slap her, using that word in such a tone when referring to him. But he caught himself. He had known Kayla ever since she had been in Jai's life. She was like family. He knew that it was just the paranoia kicking in.

"Where do you know him from?"

He moved in close to her with a serious look on his face that started to worry Kayla.

"He's just this guy I know that be at the club. I haven't heard from him in like two months. I don't know what he wants," she said, sitting back on the bed and smoking the blunt in her hand.

"Looks like he done called you like five times already," he said.

"Is this what you were trying to hide when I came outta the bathroom?"

Que moved around to the other side of the bed with the phone still in his hand while he thought about something. Why was he calling her at this time of his life? He knew that Spider worked for JoJo, who worked for Iron'RE and was considered one of the kids. They met a few times at various locations to handle business when he was in charge.

"He must be using you as a pawn," he said in a contemplating voice.

"He must be using me as a what? Boy, gimme my phone!" she yelled as she climbed to the other side of the bed to where he was.

"Hold up, hold up! Here, take your phone. When it rings again, I want you to answer it and see what he wants."

Que handed the phone back to her with no hesitation this time. He knew Kayla would do what he wanted because she knew what type of man he was. She also knew what Spider was about too. His name carried some weight in the streets. But putting him next to Que was no contest.

Just as he handed her back the phone, it rang again. This time she answered it.

"Hello!"

"Damn, baby girl! I see ya hard to get at. What you say?"

"What you want, Spider? I haven't heard from yo' ass in months. Why you blowing me up now?"

She looked at Que with a "what do I say next?" expression on her face. He rolled his hands, telling her to keep going. "What you want, Spider? Yeah, I'm busy!"

Spider got straight to the point.

"Ya still fucking with ol' boy? What's his name? Que?"

"Nah, I don't mess with that dude no more, why?" she inquired, looking over at Que.

Kayla was beginning to feel the seriousness of the conversation as it continued.

"Because, I need to get at him about some business," he told her. "Do his niece still run the club over on the west side?"

Kayla became worried at the mention of her best friend because he didn't know her like that. But Que was shaking his head, telling her on a piece of paper to tell him that she was there now and that she could find Que for him there.

Spider told her good looking and asked if he could take her out sometime soon. She went along with it by responding, "Not soon enough," before they said goodbye.

Kayla hung up the phone with dread in her eyes. The mention of her best friend's name by Spider made her antennae go up. It was the way he said it and the tone in his voice. How he asked about Que also sounded fishy. She already knew before Spider asked that she was never going out with him again.

Kayla walked over to the closet where Que had already loaded up the second gun that he was now holding in his hand while screwing on the silencer. On the floor of the closet was the first pistol that lay next to a bullet-proof vest. Kayla's eyes widened with concern.

"What's all this, babe? What's going on? Is Jai in some kind of trouble?"

She reached for his arm to turn him around so that he was

looking at her, but he didn't budge. His hands continued to fumble with the pistols and ammo, making sure that all the magazines were fully loaded and ready to go.

All this week had been a stressful one for Que. First, dealing with Iron'RE trying to chase him down and coming to the club to intimidate his niece, then killing Monte, and then the shooting at the gym. And now he done went and hired some clown to try to take him out again.

Que wasn't really worried about the clown Spider. He knew that he was just a street thug who was trying to live like those cats seen in the movies. He possessed no skills like those that he did, nor Heath or Iron'RE, for that matter.

Que almost laughed as he thought about it. Iron'RE must be sending this cat on a suicide mission. He knew that Spider couldn't mess with him when it came to killing, but what ticked him off the most was the scum mentioning the name of his niece. His whole purpose in life was to protect her, and he would do whatever was necessary to make that happen.

"Que, what's wrong? Why you got these guns and shit?"

He turned to her this time, but she had never seen this look before. It was the look of a stone-cold killer. She suddenly bagged up, putting space between them as she waited for what was next.

Que laid out the gun and magazine on the floor next to the vest. He then turned back to the closet to get dressed. He spoke to her with his back turned.

"I don't want you to go nowhere. Stay right here until I get back, and don't answer your phone while I'm gone for any reason," he ordered as he grabbed his shoes and added, "And don't mention any of this to Jai. She don't need to know anything. I'll take care of everything."

He walked over to the bed and sat down to put on his shoes. Kayla sat beside him.

"And take that boy's number outta ya phone. You won't be needing it after tonight."

When Que got into his car, he looked at the sky. Dark clouds hovered between the blue frame moving slowly across the well-lit moon as it peeked in and out, giving warning to anyone who was watching that rain was on its way.

"Perfect!" Que said to himself.

He worked well in the rain. In fact, most criminals thought that about themselves, which was why he was 100 percent sure that this idiot would show up at the club. He anticipated Spider would possibly show up with someone else to catch his niece slipping, and do whatever just to get close to him. But he would be there to make sure that didn't happen.

As Que jumped out of the car, he made a call to Jai, who was chilling at home reminiscing about her date she had with Heath. When she answered the phone, she heard the urgency in her uncle's voice.

"Unc, what's the matter?"

He told her to go to the club immediately and that everything was fine. But he needed to talk to her and told her to leave the house right away.

Anything her uncle told her to do, she would do with no questions asked. She hadn't seen Que in almost a week anyway. Once she did, she knew that she had some questions to ask him. Once she put on her shoes and grabbed her coat, she ran to her car.

"Shit, it's raining!" she said into the air.

* * *

Que was the closest, so he knew that he would get there before

Jai. Once he pulled into the lot, he saw that it was empty. He drove around the back and another time around the front to find that it was still vacant.

When he parked, he jumped out of the car with pistol in hand. He looked like a shadow as he darted for the trees that stood in the parking lot about ten meters away from where he had parked. Que had done this many times before while working for Iron'RE. His tactical skills were almost brilliant but yet certain, and he was literally untouchable.

He knew in his mind that Spider would show. That's just how stupid he knew he was. He also knew that if Iron'RE paid him, then what he paid him was motivation enough to get the job done as quickly as possible. So he would come, and Que would sit there until he did.

The rain started to come down hard, but it didn't bother Que at all as he sat poised behind the trees and focused on the front entrance to the club. The pistol was locked and loaded in his hand when he looked down to make sure. When he looked back up, he saw headlights approaching.

"Please don't be you, baby. Not yet!" he whispered to himself.

The lights were getting closer, approaching the only car parked out front. As the vehicle got closer, it slowed down, pulling right up the back of Que's vehicle's bumper to look inside. Que could see two figures. One of them climbed out from the passenger side and looked around before walking up to the car to look inside.

"Nobody in there, dawg!" he heard the guy say.

That's how close he was, and how close they were to death, Que thought to himself.

Just then, another set of headlights was approaching. Que could see that it was the Benz he had bought for his niece. His heart started to beat faster now. Not because he was scared, but because this was the one and only time that he had ever had to do some dirty where his precious niece was smack dead in the middle. The two goons saw the car approaching, and one jumped back inside their vehicle and drove a few spaces down to park.

Jai pulled right up to her uncle's car and smiled. She couldn't wait to see him and tell him about Heath.

Her mind was so distracted with Heath, Que, and the rain that when she parked and opened up her door to her car while grabbing something from the back seat, she didn't notice the figure coming up from behind her.

"Come here, bitch!" Spider yelled as he went to grab her.

She felt a hand reach for her hair and then another around her waist as she screamed trying to turn and run. But her screams were muffled by Spider's hand as he got a hold of her. She kicked and screamed as the car they were in pulled up quick with the other goon inside.

"Get her in, homie!" the other goon said. "Come on!"

They both were so distracted trying to get her into the car that they hadn't noticed Que as he slightly jogged up to them, hitting the driver from the passenger side window with two rounds. As Spider dropped Jai to the ground to get to his pistol, it was too late.

Poof! Poof! Poof!

The blast hit him in the chest and face as he fell to the ground next to Jai while she screamed for the shooter not to kill her.

Poof! Poof! Poof!

He let off three more rounds and fled to the back of the club.

When Jai saw the shooter flee, her first instinct was to run inside the club to where her uncle was. She didn't understand why he wasn't outside to protect her. But as she looked at the body lying next to her in the rain, and the guy that was slumped over in his driver's seat and apparently dead, she jumped up to run to her car and drove off, hoping to get away from this nightmare.

Once she got far enough away, she pulled over and put her head into her hands at the steering wheel and cried.

The rain continued to come down on the roof of her car as tears trickled through her fingers. She didn't notice the blood and membrane splatter from Spider's head onto the legs of her sweatpants, until she reached down into her purse to answer her phone. It was Que.

"Is everything okay? Why are you crying? Where you at?"

"Que, somebody tried to grab me!" she cried into the phone. "He killed them! He killed them, Unc! I thought that he was going to kill me too, but I ran!"

"Who, baby girl? Who tried to grab you?" he tried to sound concerned. "Where you at now?"

"I was at the club in the parking lot, and some guys tried to grab me. I was right next to your car. I thought you were in the club?"

"I am at the club. I told you to meet me here."

"I did. Then this happened!"

"I didn't hear anything."

"The guy had a silencer, because I didn't hear the shots!" she told him. "Oh, where am I? I'm in the car."

Jai was now getting her bearings as she continued to tell her uncle what had happened.

"It's two blocks right outside. He shot one dude all in the chest and face. I got his blood all over my clothes. Que," she screamed as she began to cry again. "What's going on, Que? Please tell me what's going on!"

"Jai, listen to me," he said quietly. "I want you to go home. I'll be there in a little bit. Go home and clean up. Let me go out there and check things out. Don't worry, I don't know what this is about," he lied. "But it sounds like somebody tried to rob you. I'm gonna close the club down for a minute and talk to the streets. You go home and clean up. I'll be over soon."

"Que, be careful. Please be careful!"

"I will. You just do like I told you, and I will see you later, okay?"

"Okay."

As Que hung up, he sat back in his chair to look at the surveillance. Everything was caught on tape. He watched as Spider put his filthy hands around his niece's neck, attempting to pull her into the car as she kicked and screamed.

Looking at this brought him chills as he leaned back into the chair. He then suddenly lifted back up when he saw his image coming out of nowhere, giving them the business.

"Pop! Pop!" he said in a low voice, pointing at the screen with his fingers as if he had a gun in his hands. "Stupid bastards!"

He cut off all the screens and cameras to the club as well as to the parking lot. He then hit a few buttons, and the disc came sliding out. He was now dressed in slacks under a full-length, peanut-butter-brown leather coat that fell just below his knees.

Que cut off the lights to the club before exiting through the back door. He never looked at the mess he made as he got into his car and drove off.

"Somebody will come for this trash in the morning!" he said before he turned into traffic and headed toward the freeway.

He couldn't go to Jai's right then. He didn't want her to get hurt in any way, and he knew that tonight was playing it close. He had to end this somehow, he thought as he got onto Interstate 10 and headed east. The traffic was light, so he stayed at the speed limit while cruising with the two pistols and vest on the side of him.

Ruthy B was sweeping up in the salon getting ready to open as the day showed promise for prosperity. She danced with the broom, imagining that it was her late husband, Frank, while R. Kelly's "Step" spilled from the ceiling speakers.

It had been over twenty years since her first love had been gunned down in a robbery gone bad, which left her sad and depressed for a few years. But her love carried on, and it was those feelings that she continued to carry for that man all those years that had her feeling the way she was feeling this very moment.

Alone with her thoughts, she was slightly startled when Que walked in. He stood there in the doorway and watched as Ruthy B did the step, admiring her moves at the age of seventy. She smiled when she saw that it was Que, and she reached out to give him a hug.

The place was shiny and smelled of Muslim oils, which made the customers happy when they walked in.

"Hey there, Que! Long time, no see! What brings you in here today, baby?"

Although it was a late Saturday morning, it was no surprise to see Que in a suit and tie. He seemed as comfortable as always in his loose-fitting attire.

"Dressed like a businessman," she would always say, every time she saw him, smiling ear to ear at his handsomeness.

After their embrace, she took his hand and moved to the couch where awaiting customers normally sat. As his manners forever haunted him, he waited for Ms. Ruthy B to sit down first. Once again, he kissed her on the hand before speaking.

"I was hoping to find Jai here today. Have you heard from her?"

She thought about asking him to call her, but she figured that he might have already done that.

"The last time I saw Jai was when I did her hair for her birthday," she said before she thought for another few moments. "But I did talk to her over the phone. She said that she was going to lunch with this guy she just met. Why, is everything all right?"

"Yeah, everything's cool," Que informed her while getting up to leave.

Everything was not cool, he thought to himself. But there was no reason to worry Ruthy B, because he knew how much she cared for her too.

* * *

"Oh, girl, did you hear what happened at the Catch?" Octavia said over the phone with her homegirl Kayla, telling her what she heard about what had happened to Spider. "They say the police found two bodies in the parking lot all shot up, and that one of the dudes was Spider. Don't you still mess with him?"

"Girl, I haven't seen that boy in like two months. Are you sure it was Spider though?" she asked, just to make sure.

Her mind immediately flashed to Que and the guns that she watched him leave the house with in that bullet-proof vest.

"That's what the streets say. Him and some dude named JoJo."

She knew Spider, but the second name didn't ring a bell. She felt bad for the both of them. Death was a very sad thing for her. But it was obvious that they had tried to harm her best friend, because she saw no other reason for Que to leave the house the way he had. And for that reason, she wasn't going against the grain by opening her mouth when Que told her not to.

She wanted to tell her homegirl so bad about the phone call and Que, but she held her water.

"Well, let me get off this phone. Have you talked to Jai?" she asked her friend.

Octavia hadn't talked to Jai or Que. But it wasn't strange for Jai not to call, since she was so busy. And if something had happened to her, she would have heard about it. Besides, Octavia said there were only two dead bodies, so she didn't have to worry about her friend being killed or nothing—not the way Que was protecting her.

After Octavia said that she didn't hear from her as well, they both hung up after reassuring each other that they'd talk later.

* * *

After leaving Ruthy B's Beauty Salon, Que sat in his car to contemplate. Ruthy B was helpful whether she knew it or not. The guy that his niece was seeing was indeed his ex-homeboy. With all that was going on, Que was sure that Iron'RE put this all together to try and flush him out.

Taking that money was a big mistake, and popping Monte, JoJo, and that flunky, Spider, was even a bigger one. This was because Iron'RE saw them as family, just as he once was.

But all that was thrown out the window once he crossed the line, so he knew that he had to move—and he had to move fast.

As he jumped onto Interstate 105, he headed toward Compton and made a call to his top dawg, Chub.

Chub was sitting on the porch of his gated abode when his phone rang. The birds chirped on this quiet street of ghostly neighbors with well-landscaped homes that seemed to have a sense of tranquility. But when one turned the corner, the streets came alive with all the urban activities of any other ghetto. This was where gunshots quaked the air, leaving their signature on the walls like graffiti and pumping fear into all the neighborhood locals.

"What's up, my boy?" Chub answered his phone with a smile.

He felt this way whenever he got a call from this number. Que was the reason that he was sitting pretty right now, so he knew that he would never bite the hand that fed him. At this point, he would do anything his boy Que asked of him.

"You at the crib, young Chub?"

"Yeah, I'm posted. What's up?"

"Look here, baby boy. It's barbeque or mildew. I got some meat to throw ya way. Ya got ya grill on?"

"Yeah, fo' sho! Just swing through."

"All right! Be there in a sec."

As soon as he hung up, he sat on the porch and continued to relax while bumping EZ's "Easier Said Than Done" hit from his CD player that sat beside him along with his Desert Eagle.

When Que pulled up, Chub jumped off the porch to open the gate to the driveway. Que pulled inside to join the Hummer and the '63 Chevy that was dropped to the ground with the rag down as the flakes from the paint glittered from the sun.

"What it do, baby boy?" Chub asked as Que climbed out.

The Compton sheriffs slowly passed by watching the two as they embraced.

"Awe, don't sweat them, dawg. We good on this block," he said before waving to the officers. "Come on, let's go inside."

Chub was living the life, Que thought, when he walked through the front door of his crib. The inside was even more deceiving than the outside. From the old and rugged chipped paint on the front of the house, which needed lawn work and new framing, no one could tell that he was living like Floyd Money Mayweather on the inside. The house he grew up in that was left by his mamma Anne was now an immaculate mansion on the inside.

The luxurious two-story home was equipped with all the latest technology that would even make Steve Jobs jump out of his grave. His 90-inch-screen television hung nicely above the artificial fireplace, giving life to the choice of furniture inside the living room. The kitchen was in the back of the house, where his mother used to cook some of the finest Creole meals. Her cooking would leave the house with a sweet smelling aroma. Now, the kitchen was used by Chub mostly to cook up crack cocaine.

Chub let the dogs run around the front yard once he and Que were inside. They sat at the kitchen table and watched the monitors display the front of the house while they talked business over a few shots of Hennessy.

"What's good, Que?"

"I got this problem that I need you to handle for me."

"Who is it?" Chub asked.

"This cat I know from way back. He was out the way for 'bout ten years. But now he's back, and I don't like the vibe I'm getting."

"Well, what's his name?"

"His name is Heath. I got all the info in here," Que explained as he took out a manila envelope and slid it across the table. "After I leave, take the rest of the day looking through it. Everything you need is in there."

Que took out another envelope and slid it to him.

"This is for you. It's first and last month's rent. I trust that you will take care of it on your own," he said after swallowing the last of his drink.

"Don't trip, my boy. I'll deliver you a plate when I'm done cooking."

After the two gave each other dabs, Que got into his car and drove off.

Chub put the envelope on the top of the safe while he laid back to relax. He thought about the name Heath and tried to remember where he had heard it from. He looked up at the ceiling as the blades spun from the fan.

"Where do I know this cat from?" he said to himself.

Just then his phone rang. He was able to answer it, but first he looked at the caller ID and pushed the Reject button. The T Mobil ringtone went off again before he pressed the same button to cancel the incoming call.

"Not now, Blac Chyna," he said out loud.

When it came to business like this, Chub needed no distractions. He would have to just get at Blac Chyna later. She was overrated anyway, he thought, after finally getting into her drawers. The sex was all right, but not like how the streets said it would be.

He poured himself another shot of Hennessy and set the glass onto the nightstand before getting up to retrieve the envelope with the information inside.

Once he opened it, a picture fell out.

"What the?" he said out loud as he picked it up from the floor. "Well, I'll be damned!" he added. He smiled as he looked at the familiar face.

Grabbing the second envelope that contained the twenty racks, he threw it into the safe and turned up the last of the liquid that was in his glass as he reclined back onto his bed.

* * *

It was late in the afternoon when Que decided to head home. He had a secluded spot in Rancho Cucamonga, giving him the rites of passage to Interstate 10.

As he drove in silence, he thought about the mistake he made betraying Iron'RE as well as about the danger he could have placed his niece in by coming into contact with a man who he knew could be a vicious killer if he needed to be. All of this was beginning to take a toll on him. He rubbed his temple with his trigger finger, before talking to Siri and instructing her to call his niece.

"Calling Jai now, Mr. Que," the automated voice announced.

The phone rang and rang with no answer. He tried again.

"Calling Jai now, Mr. Que."

This time it went straight to voicemail.

"What's up, Jai? Where are you at? I need to tell you something about the guy you're seeing."

His phone rang two minutes later.

"Que, what it do, my boy?" Chub said after contacting him to let him know that he was familiar with the work that he had given him. "Bro, I know this clown from Lompoc. We had an episode on the tier. I tried to stab the dude in the throat, but I missed and caught him in the arm. I caught some time behind too."

"Well, do you know where to find him?"

"He's really low-key. Hell, I didn't know he was on the streets 'til now," he replied. "But you say he stays in Long Beach, huh? He won't be that hard to find."

"Well, let me know when you're done, my boy."

"All right!" Chub said before hanging up.

After getting off the phone, Chub sat back in his recliner and fired up some of his purple haze while his pit bull, Rocco, watched. He blew smoke into the ceiling fan while looking at the picture of Heath.

"Hmmmm, so what did you do to get caught up with Que?" he said out loud. "Yeah, I won't miss this time!"

Blac Chyna came out of the bathroom in some boy shorts. She came over and straddled Chub while taking the blunt from his mouth and putting it to hers as she inhaled.

"What you doing with this pic of Jai and her new squeeze?" she asked after she exhaled and grabbed the photo from his hand.

Chub knew that he never should have let this broad in while he was conducting business, but when she had the answer to his question, he was glad that he did.

"Where you know them from?"

"That's Jai at the Catch. You know, the bi club over there on the west side."

"That's ol' girl from the swap meet that had ya all confused?" he said, snatching the blunt from her hand.

"Ain't nobody got me confused. Jai is fine as hell. I would have taken that down had you not been on my bumper."

"Shit! Look at that fat muthafucker. Who in their right mind wouldn't?" he said as he turned her around like a showcase. "Where ya know her friend from?"

"Who, Heath? He be at the sports bars downtown in Long Beach," she informed while sitting back down in his lap.

She knew not to ask questions about his business. Blac Chyna knew that Chub was in the game, and that was all she needed to know. Besides, she accepted him just as he was.

* * *

Chub went to the hydraulics shop on Artesia Boulevard to drop off his '63 Chevy. Orlie's Hydraulics was owned by Big Turtle. He had model cars of every low-rider he ever owned, showcased in a glass shelf inside the garage. He catered to all the low-riders in the city of Compton, and he even sold many overseas to China. His business was popping because everybody came to Big Turtle's.

"What's up? Something wrong with the Chevy?"

"Nah, just droppin' it off in case you wanna swing down

Broadway later on," Chub said.

"Who's that in the Humvee?"

"Oh, that's Charline aka Blac Chyna," he said as he whistled for her to come over.

When she jumped out of the Humvee, all heads turned.

"Make that thang clap, baby!" he said.

And just like that, she bent over like she was picking up some money off the ground, and let it stay there while she wiggled and clapped.

After he dropped off Blac Chyna, Chub set out to do what he got paid for. He was lucky that his girl was there at the time. She came through for him. And he showed her his appreciation before he dropped her off by buying her an expensive Rolex chain that she had around her neck by the time she got home.

After hitting up different locations, Chub found that Heath wasn't that hard to find at all. He went down to all the sports bar by Belmont Shores located near the beach, and Heath's name rang at every one.

His luck finally paid off when he sat down at the table of the last one, where he saw Heath walk through the door. He looked the same as he did when he last saw him. He was healthy and strong as a horse, which is why he had to run up on him with a shank.

"You looking good, my boy!" Chub said to himself.

When Heath jumped out of his car, he felt the handle to his 9mm pistol that was stuffed in the back of his pants, before putting on his jacket.

Since he lived in the area, he had begun to accumulate a group of friends, since he always treated the girls nicely and tipped when it was time to leave. So it was no surprise that in each sports bar, the ladies would tell him that some guy was there showing them a photo of him and asking questions. They even showed Heath some surveillance of the guy who said that he was looking for his brother, which sounded strange because many of the women, through conversing with him, knew he did not have a brother.

As he came in, he sat at the bar as usual. He told the bartender to send a drink to the empty table in the back of the bar, where he went to sit to watch the big screen in front of him.

A white server named Jennifer, who looked like Miley Cyrus, showed up for her shift and was always down for anything. She had a crush on Heath since the first time she lay eyes on him. And each time he came to the establishment, she made it her duty to serve him.

"Hey, Heath, how you doing, honey?" she asked when she brought him his drink. "You want some chicken wings with this?"

"What up, Jenn? Nah, I'm straight. But how you been though?"

"Eh, just working! Haven't seen you in a few weeks. You got lucky, huh?" she joked and winked her eye.

"You crazy, Jenn!" he said before he got serious with her. "Hey, look, do me a favor."

"Yeah, sure. Anything for you, babes."

"Ya see that guy over there in the leather coat?"

She looked to her left.

"You mean that heavy-set guy? That's the one I was telling you about."

"Yeah, good. Have you served his drinks yet?" he asked.

"He was just about to order. I was going to his table next," she told him. "What you want me to do, babes?" she questioned, leaning in so no one could hear their conversation.

Heath brought out with a few crushed pills and gave them to her.

"I want you to put these in his drink for me. Don't worry, it's all good. I got you!" he said, passing her a few bills. "Don't mention my name neither, baby girl. That's the trouble I was telling you about."

"Oh, okay, sweetie. You gonna be okay?"

"I'm good, boo," he said before she left the table.

Chub sat and watched from afar while he sipped from his drink. Heath laughed and talked on his phone while flirting with Jennifer and the other chicks as they passed by this table, not looking Chub's way at all.

"Just what are you up to?" Heath said to himself, under his fictitious laugh through his cell phone.

He still remembered the wound that Chub left from the swing of his blade. He was reminded of it each time he looked at his shoulder.

Had he not blocked it, the blade would have caught him straight in the throat.

"But that was ten years ago," he said under his breath.

When Heath looked Chub's way, Chub was starting to doze off. He could barely keep his eyes open. Now was his time to make his move. Jennifer was a beast, he thought to himself while smiling as he stood up. When he got to the table, he sat down beside him.

"Chub, my boy! Long time no see, my good friend!" he said as he put his arm around his shoulders.

"Here, let me help you up. We gotta get ya home before ya wife gets to trippin' and comes lookin' for ya ass!" he said loud enough so people could hear as they walked out the door.

He waved at the girls and blew Jenn a kiss.

"See ya, babe," he said as they disappeared.

When they got to the car, Heath took out a syringe and shot it into Chub's arm. Chub was out immediately. Heath hit the highway and then made a phone call.

* * *

Heath was in 29 Palms in two hours, just outside of Palm Springs. The road he took off of Interstate 10 led him to a shack in a deserted area. Once he got there, his headlights met up with another set of lights, which brought his car to a halt.

After turning off his lights, Heath jumped out of his car and was greeted by Candy, an old-school neighborhood toss-up.

"What's up, baby girl?" he said after giving her a kiss on the cheek.

Candy was super bad to be in her early 40s. Born in Inglewood, where all the red-bones dwelled, Candy was one that stood out from all the rest with her fat ass and bona fide breasts. She was dressed in a leather outfit that was buttoned down just below her knees.

"I'm good," she replied. "What ya got for me?"

When they went to the back seat, Chub was still slumped over.

"Help me get this clown out and get him inside," he asked.

They pulled his unconscious body from the car and carried him into the shack. Once they were inside, they threw him onto an old and stained mattress. The place was shabby and damp. Other than the mattress, there was only an old, rusty sink and toilet. Heath set up the camera that he retrieved from the trunk of his car, and then asked Candy to strip Chub down to his boxers as he lay motionless on the mattress.

"Wake yo' ass up!" Heath shouted, slapping him in the face with a wet towel.

He then turned to Candy and said, "Strip out, boo, and wear this!"

Heath threw her a ski mask and watched her put it on while he did the same.

As Candy turned on the camera and adjusted the lens so that it was focused on Chub, Heath continued to slap him with the wet towel until he came to.

"Oh, whaaat's up, man?" Chub said, barely opening his eyes.

The drugs that Heath had given him were wearing off. So when Chub saw Heath, he jumped up a bit, only to be snatched back down by the restraints.

"What the fuuuuu—!"

He couldn't get the last word out, because the wet towel smashed into his jaw.

"Who sent you?" Heath questioned.

This time he held a Taser in his hand. As Chub lay on the dirty mattress, stripped down to his underwear, his eyes widened at the sight of the Taser aimed at his nut sack.

"Who sent you?" Heath yelled again.

From the look on his face, it was obvious that he was still stunned from the drugs that Heath had given him. In fact, so much so that he didn't answer quickly enough.

"Ahhhhhh!" Chub yelled as the Taser hit him right between the legs on the thick of his thigh.

The shock sent him straight to his back.

"Ahhhh!" he yelled again as another shock from the Taser slammed into his stomach.

"I'm not gonna ask again, my boy. Who sent you?"

As Chub rolled in pain, he began to laugh. He laughed even harder when he looked at Heath, making sure that he could see his face before answering.

"You don't remember me, huh? I'm that nigga that tried to smash you on the tier at Lompoc," he laughed. "You a dead man. Somebody got a number on you, my boy!"

"Chub, I remember you," Heath admitted as he lowered the Taser to his side as he looked over at Candy. "This is the clown that stabbed me in the shoulder while we were at the Fed. Is this what this shit's about? Nigga, you ain't got nothing betta to do with ya life?

That shit's water under the bridge!"

"You don't even know, do ya?" Chub said.

"Know what?"

Chub began to laugh again as he looked at him. But then his laughter stopped as he sat back on the mattress.

"I don't know what ya did, but this dude wants you dead."

"What dude? Who you talking about?"

"My boy, I work for this dude named Que, and he wants yo' ass dead. And if I don't do it, then somebody else will. So don't trip!"

Chub couldn't see the smile on Heath's face, which was silhouetted by the light that stood between them. When he stepped back, he passed the taser to Candy. She was ready to go to work.

"Que put ya up to this?" he asked, stepping back to the video equipment. "You playing for the wrong team, bro. Que just got you murdered," Heath said as he looked over at Candy and then back at Chub. "He should have told you what type of cat I was when it comes to this killin' game."

He looked back over at Candy.

"Babe, you ready?"

"What's this bitch gonna do?"

"Oh, you don't know who Candy is. This is the homegirl right here!" Heath said as he moved in closer. "Candy, come over here and introduce yourself."

When Candy came near, she knelt down between his legs.

Through the mask, she whispered softly into Chub's ear: "Hi, baby!"

"See, Chub, I knew you were looking for me. I got eyes all around me. So when ya came down to the sports bar, my girls gave me a heads-up."

Heath then walked over to the video camera and turned it on.

"I heard that you're a sucka for big asses and tits, so I brought you a treat," he said while looking at Candy and then back to Chub. "You big ol' trick. Candy's gonna ride you real good while I film this shit and live-stream you."

And just as if on cue, Candy climbed on top of Chub and started riding him like a horse. He tried to resist, but the more he did, the more she was able to get him inside her.

"Oh, Chub!" Heath said from behind the camera, "I forgot to tell you that homegirl is HIV positive."

* * *

When Chub came to, it was almost dawn. The drugs had completely worn off, and now Chub lay on the dirty mattress shivering from the early-morning dew that made its way through the cracks of the old shack.

Heath sat on an old wooden stool riddled with holes and chipped paint, that made it look like it came out of the *National Geographic* of the Timbuktu treasures.

He waited until Chub came to. He sent Candy on her way with two racks for a job well done. Candy would have done it for free because she had a vendetta against niggas like Chub. Cats like him were the ones that had given her the virus anyway. But she thanked Heath and let him know that she was always available.

Heath wanted to get as much information from Chub as he could in order to find out where Que was hiding. He started off by scrolling through Chub's phone, but he found nothing. There was no trail leading to Que whatsoever. He threw the phone at Chub, which made a thumping sound against his stomach as it bounced off of his fluffy flesh.

"Where can I find Que at, my boy?"

At first, Heath was just going to let Candy have some fun and video them together, so that everyone that knew him would know that he got down with a broad with AIDS. But when he found out that he was sent by Que, he knew that it had just gotten real.

"How much did he pay you to kill me? I'm just curious."

Before answering, Chub looked over to where his clothes were. They lay folded neatly on the ground in the corner next to the dirty sink.

"Can I get my clothes, man? It's cold in this bitch!" he said with a smile.

"How much did he pay you?" Heath demanded.

"I ain't telling you a damn thing!"

Just then, his tone changed. He tried reaching for his clothes, but he was held back by the restraints around his legs and arms.

"He'll find out soon that I'm missing, and he'll send somebody else at yo' ass, nigga! You ain't bullet proof!"

"Oh yeah, so you're still playing hard, huh? Tell ya what. Tell me where to find Que at right now, and I'll let you go," Heath promised in all honesty.

The damage was already done, and Heath was ready to leave. He thought that throwing that bone out there would speed up the process.

He figured that Chub was one of those cats that valued his life and would do anything to come up out of a situation, even if it meant turning on his boy. But was he wrong. Young Chub held his water.

"Man, fuck you! I ain't telling you shit. You might as well kill me!"

Heath had to admire his loyalty. But still, he pulled the gun from behind his back and fired one time to Chub's head while he was still talking. His body fell back motionless.

"I already had my boy, but ya kept running your mouth. Now look at ya!" he said, stepping away from the corpse as it lay there with one eye open.

Heath got the video equipment and took it to the car, placing it in the trunk. He looked around to see that he was surrounded by nothing but desert, and thought about all the bodies that he and Que either buried or dropped in the mines that surrounded the place. He thought about Chub and went back inside to look at the body.

"You ain't even worth the time," he said out loud as he looked around to make sure that everything else was clean. "The coyotes will take care of you," he said before leaving.

Once he got to the interstate, Heath made a call to his boy

Iron'RE. He told him about the episode that had just taken place, and he then let him know that they had to get Que out of the way fast. He told him that he had taken care of the package Que had sent him. But once he found out that the package was returned to sender, it wouldn't stop him from sending another one.

"Iron'RE, I want to kill this bastard!"

"In due time, my friend. In due time. But now I want you to go home and get some rest. I'll get up with you later," he said before hanging up.

* * *

When Heath got to his house, he sat back and relaxed in the tub while thinking about everything that had just taken place. How easy it was to kill again. How easy it was to torture again. He had been out of prison a year now, and this wasn't the life he wanted to come back to—not like this. Because once he got started, he knew that it was going to be hard to stop. And right now he needed a head change, but he knew that the kush wasn't going to do it—not tonight. Tonight he needed something soft and something that smelled good. So he decided to call Jai to see if she was game to come over after he finished relaxing.

ron'RE sat in front of his laptop while Skyping with his wife in Canada, when he noticed his phone ringing. He looked at the caller ID and recognized a number he thought he would never see again.

"My love, something has come up. It's imperative that I take this call. Can I get back to you? Promise it won't take long," he said to Lisa.

Lisa blew him a kiss through the screen and said, "Promise me you'll be home soon, sweetie, will you?"

He put his hand to the screen and promised her before closing the device to answer his phone.

"Well, well! What a striking surprise. How can I help you?" he asked.

Que drove in silence without rehearsing what to say, but he knew that he had to say something in order to get his niece out of harm's way.

"Iron'RE, how can I make this right? I know I went against the grain, but there's a good explanation for my actions."

There was silence before Iron'RE responded. Que couldn't see it, but the veins in Iron'RE's neck protruded as his frustration grew with the man he once called his brother.

"Your attempt to assassinate me was flawed by the character that has become you," he said sternly. "You want to explain your actions?"

Que kept quiet as Iron'RE continued.

"Furthermore, you took away two of my kids, who were only doing what I instructed them to do. Not to mention the attempt on Heath's life!"

"I know, and I apologize for that."

"It's too late for apologies, Que. Heath is out with your niece right now awaiting instructions to snap her neck," he said with a pause. "But I may reconsider, if you surrender to me."

"Iron'RE, don't do this, man. Let me make it right."

"I've given you that opportunity. The club, remember? You have tarnished every bit of trust that I ever had in you!" he said. "Now the only way you can pay me back is with your life."

"Mr. Que, your call has been disconnected. Goodbye," the automated voice sounded.

"Oh, this feels so good. Where did you learn to do this?"

Heath let his hands continue to run down her back with some massage oil before telling her that he learned the trade during his ten-year stint at Lompoc Federal Prison while practicing on mannequins. Her eyes widened when her head shot back to look at the man that straddled her back. His hands tightened on her shoulders while his fingers rolled them back and forth. The rotation relaxed her body again as her face fell back into the pillow.

"Relax, Jai. You in good hands!" he promised. "Them days are over with."

"How come you spent so much time in prison?" Her eyes got wide again. "Did you kill someone?"

Her voice was full of excitement. She had known for a long time now that she was infatuated with the thought of someone living that type of lifestyle, where they had to kill someone. Not just the senseless killing though, but the real killings, where people got hit for being disloyal or cut-throat. She bombarded him with all kinds of questions.

"Was it a hit? How many people have you killed? Are you a gangster?" He had to smirk at the sway she said gangster though, with the "ster" instead of the "sta."

Although she hadn't seen his expression, she suddenly realized that she may have been prodding and decided not to ask any more questions.

"I'm sorry. I didn't mean to be nosey. Whatever you did, that's your business."

"It's cool!" Heath said. "Besides, you should know that I didn't go to prison for murder. Although from your response, I get the sense that you would have been delighted in me saying that I did," he said as he leaned into her ear. "In a twisted kinda way, I think you are kinda crazy."

He leaned back down and bit her ear while she giggled into the pillow.

After they made love for the third time, they both lay on top of the covers naked while looking out the glass door of the patio. The diamonds in the sky lit as they cut through the night while the air blew softly, bringing in the breeze of the salt-flavored beach that sat below the two-story condo.

"Looking out at the sky tonight is so pretty. How long have you been living here?" she asked while rubbing his chest.

"Not that long. It was sort of a gift, like a coming-home present," he said.

"Sort of, huh? Well, someone must really care for you!"

"Someone must really care for you, too, with your black 550. That's like at least seventy racks!"

"You crazy! I saw that 750 Beemer out there. What was that, a gift too?" She laughed.

"You first," he shot back at her.

"Well, my uncle bought it for me on my eighteenth birthday. It was the car I always wanted. It reminded me of a mafia carriage," she said while raising up to give him a kiss. "Now, tell me what you went to prison for. What did you do that was so bad that you had to spend ten years in there?"

This time, she moved between his legs to let her head rest on her fingers below his chest. She was ready to listen to a story that was told from the pages of his life.

He looked at her hair and said, "You really get a kick outta this

165

shit, huh?"

"What?" she responded with a whining voice that he knew he could get used to.

He took her hair and played with it between his fingers as he began to tell her about his life.

It all started with seeing his dad for the first time as a child while sitting in the front yard of his grandma's house. He saw the man that he would grow up to be like riding around on his Harley Davidson every day with a different chick. His father had been to jail so many times that his grandma told him, "Never let this kid know that you are his daddy or I'll kill ya dead, beat ass!"—her exact words. So he would come around when she wasn't watching to give Heath things from time to time.

Heath called him Uncle Harley, and his uncle was always dressed immaculately. His body was chiseled, and he always told Heath that women were the spice of life.

As he got older, the more his grandma tried sheltering him from that crazy life, the more she saw that he was becoming the same man she spent her whole life trying to keep him away from. He got the nickname Heath, short for heathen, because of all the different girls he had on any given day. The girls loved the way his body had matured after he began lifting weights. They were all over him.

He was soon abducted into the California Youth Authority where he learned how to fight. At the same time, he also enhanced his writing and verbal skills by spending his time reading books. But it wasn't long before he learned the benefits of quick cash while mastering the art of bank robbery. He watched movies like *Point Break* and *Heat*, and he imitated the characters when it came time to bounce over the counters.

Until one day, his friend was shot by a guard on the way out of the bank, which led to a high-speed chase through Chino Hills, and which later turned into a hostage situation. He was held up in what he thought was an abandoned house for at least twelve hours, holding a thirteen-year-old girl hostage until SWAT came in blazing, hitting him in the chest and collapsing one of his lungs. He died twice on his way to the hospital. When he awoke the last time, he found himself chained to a hospital bed with the cops reading him his rights.

When he finished telling his story, he looked down at Jai. She was sitting between his legs with her hands resting on his stomach now. The rain set aflame as a tear trickled its way down to her fingers. Her face stared at his, trying hard to imagine the hardship he must have endured during his journey of incarceration. How could he deal with the loneliness and all the hurt that came with being in that unwanted abyss? And to see death twice, only to come back to the reality of the disappointment of a mandatory sentence.

She began to feel empathy for this man that lay beneath her. He was strong, handsome, brave, and resilient. She saw none of this in Ricco, yet she didn't understand why she was with him for so long. She mourned his death, for she wished that upon no one. And no matter how mean he was to her, or how many times he stuck a gun down her throat threatening to kill her, she never told her uncle for fear of what he might do to him.

But right here was a real man! And because of the spell that Ricco had over her, she was unable to see her worth. It was time to let go of the past and come anew. She had to erase her past of abusiveness and paint a glorious future with someone that she thought could treat her like the queen she was. But first she had to patch the wounds of this king which lay beneath her. She realized that he had been through a lot. So she knew that the tear was for the both of them.

He put a hand to her face and wiped it away with his thumb. As the wetness dissolved, he knew that it was a mixture of pain, sorrow, betrayal, and regret. And he wished with all his might that he could make her feel better.

"What's your story, flower?" he asked, pulling her closer. "What's the tear for?"

He kissed her on the lips, then the cheek, and then on her forehead.

"It's all good. Those days are behind me," he whispered into her ear before he kissed it.

He laid her head onto his chest while they lay there in the quietness until they both fell asleep to each other's heartbeat.

When she awoke, she felt an excruciating pain around her neck. She could barely breathe, gasping for air as her eyes looked frantically at the ceiling. The room was the same place in which she fell asleep hours ago on the chest of the man that brought her comfort. But now it seemed that she was in a lock by the same arms that had embraced her.

Her eyes rolled to the back of her head as she tried screaming his name. And as the peak sound reverberated, Heath suddenly awoke, finding Jai's head locked tightly between his arms. Hurriedly, he released her, turning her body to him so that he could see her face. The tears fell down as she tried to figure out what the hell had just happened. She looked at her clothes on the floor and thought about grabbing them to leave. But the perplexed look on his face convinced her that something crazy was going on with him, and her feelings would not let her leave until she found out what it was.

"I'm sorry. I must've had a nightmare!" he said. "Are you okay?"

Heath could see that she was nervous by the way her body was shaking. He kissed her on the cheek and then on the forehead. She looked at him with eyes of uncertainty, but then a frantic smile appeared on her face. He took her hand into his and kissed it.

"I've been having these nightmares ever since I got out of prison. I didn't mean to hurt you. Normally there's nobody in my bed like this."

Jai leaned back, positioning herself on his chest, and said, "I can see why. Them other chicks must be lucky. It must have been rough in there. Ten whole years!"

She let out a deep breath and then turned her body so that her breast lay softly on his chest. She looked into his eyes. They were strong and stern. She could tell that something was on his mind.

"How did you survive in there? I mean, I see that you're strong physically," she began, grabbing his arm with her small hands, barely wrapping them around. "But mentally. How did you handle all that?"

She laid the back of her head into his chest this time. She was comfortable now. And though the questions seemed personal, she felt that he owed her the answer after nearly choking her to death.

"I mean, I couldn't imagine being locked up in one of them cells for ten years doing nothing. It must've been scary in there at times," she questioned. "I mean, not like scary like somebody messing with you scary. Because I'm pretty sure that you could handle your own, but didn't you get lonely?"

When she reached for one of his hands, they were balled into a fist. She could feel the tension, realizing that she might have said too much. But when she looked up, she was relieved to see the smile that met her face with a kiss.

"Damn, babe, I can see that you can go on and on with these

questions."

He kissed her again. This time, by cupping her chin with the most gentle touch before whispering, "You have no idea how bad that place could get; and right now that's not a place I want to take you."

He pulled her to his chest and wrapped his arms around her.

Her phone went off. As she broke from the embrace, she reached over the side of the bed until she found it under her clothes. The caller ID read: "Uncle Que."

She answered on the third ring as Heath got up to grab a fresh pair of boxers. He was on his way to the shower when he heard his name. He then stopped dead in his tracks while the love of his life spoke through her phone.

"But, Que, how long will you be gone? I haven't seen you in a minute. I can't stop by and give you a hug before you go!"

There was silence on the other end as Heath listened for her to respond. She nodded before saying okay, then silence again. Heath eased back to the bed to kiss her on the shoulder so that he could eavesdrop on their conversation. He wanted to snatch up the phone and tell Que that he had his niece and could do anything he wanted with her unless he showed up to receive his retribution. In fact, he couldn't understand why he wasn't doing that right now, tying her to the bed and gagging her while Que listened, and telling him where to find Chub's body. The shock in his voice would be satisfying, he thought.

Suddenly, he heard his name. The words came softly from her lips. She had this devious look in her eyes when she saw her reflection in the mirror, and as she turned around with the phone in hand, Heath grabbed it. He spoke with the phone in one hand while holding Jai with the other.

His grip on her became harder as he flashed back to his old life. But as he looked into her eyes to witness the fear, his mind suddenly flashed to the future, and where he was seeing his life with this woman. He realized that he had fallen in love.

"Que," he began, releasing his grip as Jai jumped onto the bed and wrapped her arms around her knees. "Don't worry, we have no interest in doing nothing to her. Iron'RE only wants to speak with you."

He looked at Jai while Que spoke into the phone. She couldn't hear a thing. She just sat there and watched as Heath listened. He wished that he could make her understand, but now wasn't the time.

"Why would you betray ya boy like that?" he questioned as he jumped up and began to pace the floor.

He was sure that Jai wouldn't move. She seemed still confused about her feelings. Part of her felt betrayed, while the other part of her felt frightened.

"Close to a mil ya stole, Que, and for what?"

He walked over to the patio door and looked outside. The ocean moved with force. He turned back around to see the look on Jai's face, but he couldn't because her face was still buried between her knees.

"What ya do that for, dawg? He would have given you that! What happened to ya, bro?"

After a long silence, Que finally spoke.

"I don't expect you to understand. You been gone for a decade. Times have changed. People have changed," he said before he paused and said, "I have changed."

"But, Que, Iron'RE loved you like a brother. Why didn't ya just ask him for the money? You been working for him for years. Why throw all that away?"

"When you went away, things got tough. Iron'RE was in trouble with the Feds. They were trying to move on him."

"He never told me anything like that!"

"That's because he was trying to protect you. He didn't want any Fed knocking at ya cell door. You already had ten to walk off."

"So what happened?" Heath asked.

"Well, after you left, he put me in charge of the money. I oversaw the kids, the wife, and everything that required financial stability," he started as he walked around to the driver's side of his car, which was parked outside of Heath's condo. "I know you've been seeing Jai for a minute now. I spotted you two at the Sizzler."

"And what's that got to do with anything? She has nothing to do with this!"

"But she does. I know Iron'RE too well. He sent you to get at my niece in order to get close to me."

Heath looked back at Jai as Que continued.

"And I know this because I've been following her this whole time."

Que looked up at the building.

"I know Iron'RE wouldn't do anything to harm her. That's rule number one. Never do harm to women or children."

"Why did you take the money then? What, you get greedy?"

"Stupid! You think I took the money because of greed? Is that what you think this is about?"

Jai still had her knees to her chest, staring down at the bed. Heath went to touch her, but she jumped at the very thought of being touched by a man who had invaded her space.

The two of them looked through the bedroom doorway when they heard the knock coming from the front door of the condo. Jai thought to break and run, but she then spotted her clothes that were still on the floor.

Heath continued his conversation with Que as he walked through the doorway to see who was at the front door. His mind was so occupied with the issue at hand that he didn't notice the intrusion. He opened the door to a man with a chromed Desert Eagle pointed straight at his head.

The man behind the trigger had a familiar face from a time that once was. He then made his way inside with the gun still in hand. He told Heath to have a seat on the couch as he closed the door behind him. Heath thought about resisting, because he knew that he could probably take him with one swift move. But from the looks of it, he knew that Que was in no hurry to do him harm, or else he would have already. If anything, he just wanted to make sure that his niece was straight.

Once she heard her uncle's voice, Jai emerged from the bedroom fully dressed with tears streaming down her face. The tears were not because of fear, but because of the twisted feelings that she was having for this man who had just caused all this confusion. She moved quickly to her uncle's side as he reached for her face to dry her tears.

"Are you okay, sweetheart?"

Her eyes gave him the answer as he turned back toward Heath with the Desert Eagle still on him. He went to fire, but it was too late. With one swift kick, Heath knocked the gun from his hands and it fell to the floor. They wrestled while throwing blows as Heath countered with a swift blow to the gut and a series of combos to the face, before Que could get out of the way. Que was almost unconscious when Heath grabbed him by his shirt collar.

"Why did you take the money?" he asked again as he held him down. "What happened to ya, man?"

Que smiled as the blood stayed in the corner of his mouth. It was hard, but he managed it. He knew that his jaw was fractured from the pain when he smiled, but Heath couldn't tell what he was thinking.

"I gotta call Iron'RE," he said as he picked up the phone from the floor where Que lay. "Ya know he's gonna kill ya."

Pop! Pop!

Two shots rang from the Desert Eagle. Heath jumped. When he turned around, he saw Jai with the gun in hand ready to bust again as she came closer.

"Get away from him, or I swear, Heath, I'll kill you!"

Her grip on the handle was stern. Although she was a little distraught, Jai seemed to maintain her composure.

Heath stared at her as he inched his way to the door.

"Wait a minute, Jai. You gotta listen to me. I never meant for you to get hurt."

"Did you know that he was my uncle? Did you use me to get close to him?" she yelled, her hands shaking now as she looked at Que.

"Jai!" Que shouted, "Listen to me. He works for a man named Iron'RE. He's the guy with the Mongolian that I was telling you about."

"The guy that came to the club? The guy in the suit?" she asked while staring at Heath. "What is this all about? Why are you and this guy looking for my uncle?"

"I used to work for him," Que responded. "He was a very close friend to the both of us."

Jai was confused and lowered the gun down to her side as she looked at Heath.

"Back in the day, me and Heath did some jobs for this man. He took care of us."

"She doesn't need to hear all this, Que," Heath said as he stood in his boxers at the door now, debating on whether to make a move on the gun that was still in Jai's hand.

"Iron'RE is a crime boss," he continued. "He's the reason that I was able to take care of you all these years."

"Let that go, dawg!" Heath warned.

"Heath was the one I brought in to work for Iron'RE, figuring that I owed him that much for him nearly saving my life."

Jai looked at Heath with glassy eyes.

"Soon, after Heath went to jail, I took over everything while Iron'RE sat back and enjoyed life. He gave me control of everything." He looked at Heath. "I admit it. I did get a little greedy," he said as he looked from Heath to Jai. "But it was all for you, baby girl."

Que sat up from the floor and rubbed his jaw as the blood dripped from his lips.

The gun was again aimed at Heath.

"How was this all for me, Que? Why would you do this all for me? I never asked for any of this!" Jai questioned as she lowered the gun now as her eyes went to the floor.

Heath was about to make a move, but he hesitated. He saw that some dirt was about to unfold, so he waited and listened.

"When you and your brother were born, your mother, Kathy, was so happy. You were two of the most beautiful babies the world had ever seen. But then your brother got sick, and your mother blamed the doctor that delivered you. I tried to tell her that it wasn't the doctor's fault. Your brother only had a piece of his heart that pumped the little life that he had, but she wasn't buying it. We tried everything, but your brother was getting sicker by the day. Then they found out about a procedure that might have worked. Because you were twins, it was best to use some of your tissue from your heart to see if it would help him. But it never got to that point, because the day of the operation, right as the doctor was cutting you open, your brother passed away. It was almost as if he was saying that he didn't want you to go through the pain. Your body was so small. You were only a year old, which is probably why you don't remember."

This time she dropped the gun and fell to the floor sobbing. She rubbed the long thick scar that she had had to live with all her life, not knowing that it was an attempt to help her brother live. She reached for the gun and aimed it at Que.

"Say my mother's name again, you lying piece of shit!"

The sobs came harder.

"You said that my mother's name was Kathy. My Aunt Kathy? Auntie Kathy was my mother? Why all the lies, Que?"

"After your brother died, your mother went to the hospital to confront the doctor. But when she got there, so much rage came over her that she shot him right between the eyes."

Que crawled to Jai and reached for the gun, but she tossed it to Heath.

"Shoot this lying piece of shit!" she pleaded.

"Listen to me, baby girl!" he said as he threw up his hands at

Heath. "Wait a minute! She needs to hear this."

Heath pointed the gun at his head.

"We moved you to Oakland because your mom was on the run for murder, and I was an accessory to murder because I waited for her in the parking lot. I didn't know that she was gonna kill that dude until she came running out to the car crying and carrying the smokin' gun. You were only five when your mother couldn't take it no more," he said. "She killed herself, and that's when you came to LA."

"You told me that she died of natural causes, you liar!"

Jai got up from the floor and moved closer to Heath.

"You said that my Aunt Kathy was my mother. That makes you my father!"

"Which is why I tried so hard to take care of you," he answered.

"I made sure that Ruthy B looked over you each time I went outta town, and served you big for each birthday party you had. And I never forgot about Jarrod. I had to do this all from afar, because the Feds were looking for me. They've now been on me tough, which is why I had to make a move."

Que got up to his feet while Heath still had the gun pointed at his head.

"So your name isn't really Quency?"

"Nah, it's Arthur. Your mother and I named you Jai Rambsey after her. Kathy was the name she took on after all this had happened," Que admitted. "I'm sorry, baby girl."

He reached for her, but she pulled away. Heath then looked over at him.

"So this whole thing was to get another identity and get lost again. Why didn't you just tell Iron'RE? He would have hooked you up."

"As much as he had going on, there was just so much dirt! The last thing I wanted to do was bring the Feds his way."

"So you'd rather just jack him instead?"

"I know that wasn't the way. I mean, he gave me a way out when we bought the club."

Jai looked at him. "You bastard! That club is his!"

"The club was the both of ours," Que said. "I had to pay him back in percentage. But once we started, I got cold feet. Plus, the Feds were getting close."

"So what's your plan?" Heath asked. "Were you going to leave your daughter behind?"

183

Que looked over at Jai.

"Once I knew that you were following her, I stopped by Ruthy B's to see if Jai had spoken about you and how she felt about you. I knew that you were with her tonight. And I can see that you care for her a lot."

Heath lowered the gun.

"At first, Iron'RE sent me out to hunt you down to kill you. It went as far as getting close to your daughter just to lead me to you," he began, putting his arm around Jai, who was still looking perplexed. "But then I fell in love with her. Iron'RE knew that I wasn't in the life no more, but I felt I owed him this one. He took care of me the whole time I was down, and then some."

Heath looked around the room just as his phone began to ring. From the ringtone, he knew exactly who it was. The text message read: "I'm at the front door."

Iron'RE walked inside. He was dressed in the same style suit with his Mongolian hanging down his back. Although Heath's condo was immaculate in its décor, Iron'RE took precedence over his surroundings as he unbuttoned his suit jacket to expose the two Berettas that sat in holsters under his armpits.

When he reached the couch, he saw that Que was handcuffed. He sat next to him completely poised.

"How's a brother?" he asked, not needing a reply. "I know about your secrets," he began, grabbing his freshly braided Mongolian. "But what I don't know is why you didn't come to me instead of stealing. You're a thief, Que?"

Iron'RE then turned to Jai.

"I want to apologize for the way that I introduced myself earlier. As you can see, I am a man of honor and like to honor those who are worthy."

He next looked over at Heath.

"And you, my brother, are my friend for life. I hate that I had to interrupt your program for this nonsense," he said while looking over at Que, "but I owe you, bro."

Jai looked at Heath while Iron'RE continued to speak. Although her life had been a lie, she knew that she didn't want her father to die. Her aunt? Her uncle? Who was she really? But as all this circulated through her brain, she knew who she really wasn't—and that was a killer!

She tried to persuade Heath to cash in his card of favors to see if he could do anything to save her father, now that the truth was out. Jai knew that it would take the rest of her life to find out who she truly was, and she knew that she would need her father to help her do so. She grabbed Heath by the hand.

"I think I love you!"

The words just fell out of her mouth like chewed food. She was surprised when she said it, and so was Heath.

"You think? You gotta do better than that, Flower!"

"If I do, will you convince your friend not to harm my unc . . . I mean my father?"

She looked over at him. Iron'RE sat, still poised as he calmly talked to Que almost in a whisper.

"I love you, Heath. I think I knew that when I woke up in your arms," she admitted, squeezing his hand tightly. "My father seems to have made a lot of mistakes, but it was because of me. He did it to be there for me," Jai said loud enough for Iron'RE to hear her.

"What do you think I should do with him, young lady?"

Jai looked over at Iron'RE and then to her father before speaking.

"Well, the club is doing good. He could pay you back that way. I will continue to run it, and you can pick up the cash until it's paid in full."

"That's fine," he said. "But there's still the issue of your father stealing from me in the first place."

Jai let go of her new love and walked over to her father. She knew from the way that Iron'RE looked at her that the floor was hers—and that her father's fate relied on her forgiveness. She knelt down beside him.

"Mr. Arthur, today you have devastated me. You have lied to me and put me in harm's way, and yet I still love you, and I don't want anything to happen to you." She stood back up. "Either way, after today, I might not see you ever again." She looked back at Iron'RE. "I think you should let him go. You could get him another identity and move him out of the country."

Iron'RE rubbed his face as he contemplated her suggestion. When he looked at Que, he smiled.

"You have a remarkable young lady for a daughter. Too bad you missed the opportunity of being a father to her."

When Iron'RE got up, he walked over to Jai and wrapped his arm around her.

"Anything you need, don't hesitate to ask. After your father disappears, there will be no more contact between the two of you. If this is going to be done, it must be done right."

He then walked over to Que.

"I will have to fake his death and move him to India with my family. And you will become my adopted daughter, if that's all right with you," he said, looking back at Jai with a smile.

CHAPTER NINETEEN

The Happy Ending

Octavia and Kayla sat around the bar while Jai poured them a drink. It was in the middle of the day that the three enjoyed each other's company while discussing Jai's latest circumstances. They were surprised to find out that Que was her father, but even more surprised that he had suddenly died in a horrific car accident, which went up in flames before rescue arrived. The burning vehicle, or what was left of it, left no sign of life except for the ashes of skeletal remains of the two occupants that could only be identified by their IDs that miraculously survived the fire.

Another toast was made to Jai and her fiancé, who had just walked through the door. Kayla and Octavia had a jaw-dropping moment when they saw the man of their best friend's dreams all decked out in his Armani suit and clean cut. As he walked past them, Heath couldn't help but remember the fun time he had under the covers with her homegirls. And as they looked at each other, they all silently agreed to keep the episode among the three of them.

"Ladies," he said.

"Heath." They giggled in unison as Jai looked at them acting like silly little teens.

She reached out to hug her new squeeze and knew this was where she wanted to be. Right here in his arms.

Heath drove in silence as he reflected on the past. He thought about the lifestyle that he once lived with Iron'RE, vowing never to turn that way again. He thought about giving back and contemplated as to how. And when he heard about his nephew getting out, he vowed to snatch him up once he got home so that he could teach him to become a man.

Exavier was seventeen now. His three years at the Juvenile Hall Detention Center were coming to an end as the system was getting ready to throw him back to the wolves of the concrete jungle.

At age fourteen, he came in as wild as a beast with so many insecurities, that trust was thrown out the window. He fought every day, always in the hole. And his rehabilitation was limited due to his discipline problems, because he had none.

Exavier lost his father to a senseless murder while incarcerated. His confidence was shattered when he got the news that his dad was struck in the head by crossfire with a young Black kid and the police on the corner of 108th Street and Western Avenue as he was coming out of the store.

When Heath got the news from his sister that Exavier was coming home, he knew that he had to grab him so that he didn't end up in prison as an adult like he did. That was one of the reasons that so many Black men ended up in the system, because they had no father in their lives to coach them.

When Exavier came home, Heath was determined to make it happen, not because of his sister's request, but because he knew that it was the right thing to do.

"I got ya, nephew," he said to himself as he let the 750 float up the interstate.

* * *

Exavier was anxious around June 23, because he knew this was the day he would be getting out of this hell hole. Since the three years had passed, Exavier grew from a frail little kid into a handsome young man. He stood six-foot-tall with about two hundred plus pounds of flesh and muscle, which were well fitting for his deep Barry White voice. The system would do that to you, with all the starched food they feed you and the daily weight-lifting regimen. You can't miss how fast one of these youngsters can grow.

Heath was shocked when he saw his nephew walk through the

gates in a brown khaki suit and white T-shirt. The last time he had seen Exavier, the kid was only six years old, but now look at him! He was a beast, Heath thought to himself.

"Damn, nephew! What was they feedin' you in there?" he asked.

Jumping out of his car to embrace the kid, Heath was shocked some more at the sound of his nephew's voice when he responded.

"Who are you? You gon' get all the honeys with a tune like that one! Come on, let's get you outta here!" Heath said before he frowned at the khaki suit he looked at as they jumped into the car. "We gotta get ya some new gear."

Exavier was relieved to be home. It was such a dark place in there, he thought as he looked out the window to catch the trees dancing in the wind. It was as if God was blowing on them telling them, "Rejoice, for your time has come." But for him, he knew that the struggle wasn't over. His difficulties would always continue throughout his life's journeys. So as he cruised with his uncle up the interstate, he admired the grained wood and the soft reception of the upholstered leather, which made him feel like the president for the time being.

"This is a bad-ass car, Uncle Heath! How you get this shit?" he

3

questioned with his eyes wide.

"A gift from a friend, nephew. That's what it is. Ya show love to ya soldiers when they come home," he said. "Just like I'm gonna show you. You earned it!"

"What you talking about?"

"We going to the swap meet to get ya fitted, young dude. You gonna need some gear," he repeated, looking over at his attire. "Them chicks gonna be on you," he said as he looked down at his feet and smiled. "What size shoe you wear?"

"What?" Exavier replied.

The question went over his head, and his uncle knew it. He laughed while scanning his playlist until he found the track he was looking for and pressed play.

"Don't trip, nephew. I'll lace you later," he said as Dr. Dre's 2001 *Chronic* album banged through his woofers. "Besides, when we get finished shopping, we gotta sit down and have a man-to-man, because I don't need ya going back to that place."

Exavier looked out the window again at trees and cars as they passed by with people inside who were just like him: free. He looked at the clouds and saw a plane carrying passengers from somewhere back to LAX Airport, before turning back to his uncle.

"Unc, I ain't never going back to jail."

"That's what's up. But ya know there are all kinds of temptations out here. Ya gotta stay on ya toes," Heath reminded him.

He then looked at him as he modulated the tunes to make sure that Exavier understood what he was about to say next.

"I hear you like to fight."

* * *

Exavier lay back on the couch while playing Play Station 4 with his new Jordans on. He had no idea what he was going to do with his life. His only concern at the moment was Mayweather trying to kill Pacquiao with some vicious uppercuts as he pushed the buttons to the controller. It reminded him of all the ungloved bouts that he had to endure during his incarceration. In each one, he came out on top as his skills enhanced, just like this boxing game with each round.

It suddenly dawned on him what he wanted his profession to be as he had Manny Pacquiao against the ropes, giving him blow after blow. He smiled while inching up from the couch, anxiously coming to his feet as the referee started the countdown while his contender was laid out on the canvas.

"Eight . . . nine . . . ten!" the Play Station 4 ref announced as he threw up his hands. "Knock out!"

Exavier threw the control to the floor as he leaned back on the couch to look up at the ceiling. He relaxed, letting his eyelids close for a minute.

"I wanna be a boxer. That's what I'm gonna do!" he announced as he opened his eyes to grab his phone and make a call.

He stopped at the third number, hesitated, and then started dialing again before a tear escaped. It rang twice before someone picked up. He listened as the beautiful voice that he was all too familiar with reverberated through the answering machine

"This is Dena. I'm unable to come to the phone right now, so please leave a message." Beep!

"Hello, Mom. I'm out! I'm free! Uncle Heath picked me up and bought me all kinds of clothes. I finally know what I'm gonna do, Mom. I'm gonna be a boxer!" he announced as the tears came rolling down his face. "I wish you were here, Mom. First Dad, and now you! I wish you were alive to see how much your son has grown. I love you, Mom!"

He threw the phone onto the couch as he wiped away the tears from his face. He wished that he could have made it home before his mother departed, so that she could see the change. He was no longer the problem child, although he was still with the business. He had become everything rehabilitation defined. And though he still suffered from ADHD, Exavier managed to escape discipline whenever his behavior got out of hand. He learned to channel that energy into working out as his body continued to mature as well as his mind. And now that he was home, he wanted his mom to witness his refinement. But his mom had supposedly fallen short to the cravings of meth, with the drug taking over her mind and, soon after, her body.

Exavier remembered getting the news while he was lifting weights out on the yard. His youth counselor, Mr. Wilson, came outside to call him into his office for an important phone call. It was his Uncle Heath on the other end letting him know that his mother had been found dead inside a motel room.

Her throat had been slashed while the assailant left her to bleed out. Exavier wanted to flash and take out his frustrations on someone, but he did not. He just continued to listen.

"Nephew, I got you when you come home. I'll take care of you.

7

Don't trip!"

Later that day, Exavier lay in his bunk with a picture of his beautiful mother, one with her sober while holding his little body in her arms at six months old. Tears ran down his face that night as he curled up into a fetal position, silently making a promise to find his mother's killer and make him pay.

Text Good2Go at 31996 to receive new release updates via text message.

To order books, please fill out the order form below:
To order films please go to www.good2gofilms.com

Name: __ _____

Address:_____

City: _____ State: _____ Zip Code: _____

Phone:_____

Email:_____

Method of Payment: Check   VISA   MASTERCARD

Credit Card#:_ _____

Name as it appears on card: _____

Signature: _____

Item Name	Price	Qty	Amount
48 Hours to Die – Silk White	$14.99		
A Hustler's Dream - Ernest Morris	$14.99		
A Hustler's Dream 2 - Ernest Morris	$14.99		
A Thug's Devotion – J. L. Rose and J. M. McMillon	$14.99		
Black Reign – Ernest Morris	$14.99		
Bloody Mayhem Down South – Trayvon Jackson	$14.99		
Bloody Mayhem Down South 2 – Trayvon Jackson	$14.99		
Business Is Business – Silk White	$14.99		
Business Is Business 2 – Silk White	$14.99		
Business Is Business 3 – Silk White	$14.99		
Childhood Sweethearts – Jacob Spears	$14.99		
Childhood Sweethearts 2 – Jacob Spears	$14.99		
Childhood Sweethearts 3 - Jacob Spears	$14.99		
Childhood Sweethearts 4 - Jacob Spears	$14.99		
Connected To The Plug – Dwan Marquis Williams	$14.99		
Connected To The Plug 2 – Dwan Marquis Williams	$14.99		
Connected To The Plug 3 – Dwan Williams	$14.99		
Deadly Reunion – Ernest Morris	$14.99		
Dream's Life – Assa Raymond Baker	$14.99		
Flipping Numbers – Ernest Morris	$14.99		
Flipping Numbers 2 – Ernest Morris	$14.99		
He Loves Me, He Loves You Not - Mychea	$14.99		
He Loves Me, He Loves You Not 2 - Mychea	$14.99		
He Loves Me, He Loves You Not 3 - Mychea	$14.99		
He Loves Me, He Loves You Not 4 – Mychea	$14.99		
He Loves Me, He Loves You Not 5 – Mychea	$14.99		

Lord of My Land – Jay Morrison	$14.99		
Lost and Turned Out – Ernest Morris	$14.99		
Married To Da Streets – Silk White	$14.99		
M.E.R.C. - Make Every Rep Count Health and Fitness	$14.99		
Money Make Me Cum – Ernest Morris	$14.99		
My Besties – Asia Hill	$14.99		
My Besties 2 – Asia Hill	$14.99		
My Besties 3 – Asia Hill	$14.99		
My Besties 4 – Asia Hill	$14.99		
My Boyfriend's Wife - Mychea	$14.99		
My Boyfriend's Wife 2 – Mychea	$14.99		
My Brothers Envy – J. L. Rose	$14.99		
My Brothers Envy 2 – J. L. Rose	$14.99		
Naughty Housewives – Ernest Morris	$14.99		
Naughty Housewives 2 – Ernest Morris	$14.99		
Naughty Housewives 3 – Ernest Morris	$14.99		
Naughty Housewives 4 – Ernest Morris	$14.99		
Never Be The Same – Silk White	$14.99		
Shades of Revenge – Assa Raymond Baker	$14.99		
Slumped – Jason Brent	$14.99		
Someone's Gonna Get It – Mychea	$14.99		
Stranded – Silk White	$14.99		
Supreme & Justice – Ernest Morris	$14.99		
Supreme & Justice 2 – Ernest Morris	$14.99		
Supreme & Justice 3 – Ernest Morris	$14.99		
Tears of a Hustler - Silk White	$14.99		
Tears of a Hustler 2 - Silk White	$14.99		
Tears of a Hustler 3 - Silk White	$14.99		
Tears of a Hustler 4- Silk White	$14.99		
Tears of a Hustler 5 – Silk White	$14.99		
Tears of a Hustler 6 – Silk White	$14.99		
The Panty Ripper - Reality Way	$14.99		

The Panty Ripper 3 – Reality Way	$14.99		
The Solution – Jay Morrison	$14.99		
The Teflon Queen – Silk White	$14.99		
The Teflon Queen 2 – Silk White	$14.99		
The Teflon Queen 3 – Silk White	$14.99		
The Teflon Queen 4 – Silk White	$14.99		
The Teflon Queen 5 – Silk White	$14.99		
The Teflon Queen 6 - Silk White	$14.99		
The Vacation – Silk White	$14.99		
Tied To A Boss - J.L. Rose	$14.99		
Tied To A Boss 2 - J.L. Rose	$14.99		
Tied To A Boss 3 - J.L. Rose	$14.99		
Tied To A Boss 4 - J.L. Rose	$14.99		
Tied To A Boss 5 - J.L. Rose	$14.99		
Time Is Money - Silk White	$14.99		
Tomorrow's Not Promised – Robert Torres	$14.99		
Tomorrow's Not Promised 2 – Robert Torres	$14.99		
Two Mask One Heart – Jacob Spears and Trayvon Jackson	$14.99		
Two Mask One Heart 2 – Jacob Spears and Trayvon Jackson	$14.99		
Two Mask One Heart 3 – Jacob Spears and Trayvon Jackson	$14.99		
Wrong Place Wrong Time – Silk White	$14.99		
Young Goonz – Reality Way	$14.99		
Subtotal:			
Tax:			
Shipping (Free) U.S. Media Mail:			
Total:			

Make Checks Payable To:
Good2Go Publishing
7311 W Glass Lane,
Laveen, AZ 85339

CPSIA information can be obtained
at www.ICGtesting.com
Printed in the USA
LVHW021446080219
606907LV00016B/460/P